# RAIN OF FIRE

///////

Osborne saw the tracers rocket by the cockpit. Glowing red balls that disappeared into the cloud deck. He rolled over and hit the trigger for the cannons. Below him the ground was erupting. Men shooting upward as the Wild Weasels dived on the targets. Rockets tore up the ground as the twenty-millimeter cannon chewed up real estate. There was return fire and then secondary explosion.

"I got a SAM site to the right. Weasel Four."

Osborne had no idea where Weasel Four was. The flight had gotten separated by the enemy. He pulled back on the stick and climbed high, toward the cloud deck, looking back the way he'd come. Through the mist and fog, he could see a couple of fires burning, but he couldn't see the other two jets.

"Got a SAM site to the four o'clock," said Kenyon.

Without thinking, Osborne turned toward it. He pushed on the stick and started his dive...

# WINGS OVER NAM 2
## THE WILD WEASELS

ALSO BY CAT BRANIGAN

Wings Over Nam #1:
CHOPPER PILOT

Wings Over Nam #3:
LINEBACKER*

**Published by**
**POPULAR LIBRARY**     *forthcoming

# WINGS OVER NAM #2

## THE WILD WEASELS

## Cat Branigan

**POPULAR LIBRARY**

An Imprint of Warner Books, Inc

A Warner Communications Company

POPULAR LIBRARY EDITION

Popular Library® and the fanciful P design are registered trademarks of
Warner Books, Inc.

Cover art by Cliff Miller
Cover design by Jackie Merri Meyer

Popular Library books are published by
Warner Books Inc.
666 Fifth Avenue
New York, N.Y. 10103

 A Warner Communications Company

Printed in the United States of America

First Printing: September, 1989

10  9  8  7  6  5  4  3  2  1

## Author's Note

This is a highly fictionalized account of the development of the Wild Weasel program and the deployment of that system to Vietnam in the mid-1960s. In the story I have taken liberties with the truth, but the underlying theme, and certainly the bravery of the men flying the Wild Weasels, is not fiction. It is my hope that the men who flew the Wild Weasels will view this work as a tribute to their courage and ingenuity. It is meant to be that.

# ONE

A T ten thousand feet and four miles off the coast of South Vietnam, the flight of four F-105 fighters was safe. It had been almost two years since the North Vietnamese air force had flown south of the DMZ, and the triple-A and SAM sites were a fixture in the north, not the south. So, at ten thousand feet, with the South China Sea spread out beyond, sparkling like some gigantic jewel, there was very little to worry about. Just keeping the flight together and watching the instruments. A long, straight, and level flight that wouldn't get interesting until it was time to cross the coastline and enter North Vietnamese airspace.

Air Force Major William Taylor sat sweating in the cockpit, squinting in the bright sunlight. Sweat soaked his face and tried to drip into his eyes, but the sweatband he wore defeated it. His shoulders were stiff, his hand was cramped, and he hadn't been airborne that long. He and the flight of four had come off the runway at Tan Son Nhut, rendezvoused with a KC-135 tanker for a long, deep drink, and then headed north. Normally the fighter-bombers that attacked into the north were from bases in Thailand or closer to the DMZ, like Da Nang, or from carriers off Yankee Station in the South China Sea, but once in a while a super effort was put together and fighters based deep in South Vietnam got to fly north. Taylor wasn't sure that he appreciated the opportunity.

Taylor was a tall, slender man with black hair and a heavy beard that required him to shave twice a day. He had light, white skin that seemed to resist the tropic sun he hated. From the minute he got up, usually sometime before sunrise, until the moment he went to bed, he stayed out of the sun. If he didn't, he burned quickly and badly. He was one of the few men who had been in South Vietnam for more than a month who had not acquired a deep, dark tan.

Like many of the others who found themselves flying in Southeast Asia, he had not started out to get there. A fine student in high school as well as a good athlete, he had secured an appointment to the Air Force Academy and then, with the other top graduates, he had gone on to flight school. The war that was beginning in Vietnam was so unimportant that many of his fellows hadn't heard about it. Taylor thought there might be a chance for some real combat flying in Vietnam, though the story was that the Air Force pilots in Vietnam were there just to train the South Vietnamese.

Then came the Gulf of Tonkin incident, and the politicians had their excuse to send in American combat troops. The charade of advisors and combat instructors was gone. There were no South Vietnamese pilots in the flight that Taylor led now, heading toward the north. South Vietnamese pilots didn't fly into the north. Ever. And that was just fine with Taylor and all the other Americans. It meant that they didn't have to watch their backs as they flew.

This was the second best time of the mission. The peace and quiet of flying high above the trouble, far outside the ranges of the enemy weapons systems, with an AWACS plane orbiting high overhead watching for enemy fighters, made it relaxing. If anything came off the ground in North Vietnam, Taylor and every other flight leader heading into battle would be alerted. Once the fighters crossed into North Vietnam, such warnings would be useless since the planes would probably be engaged by the time the warning was given. But now, over the South China Sea, there wasn't anything to do but fly the airplane and watch the clouds building in the deep blue of the sky.

Taylor shot a glance at his wingman in the number two position and then turned, looking at the second element lead in the number three slot. Both were up tight, hanging close to him. A good, tight formation. Not the sloppy thing it would have been with the South Vietnamese flying with them.

He then looked down at the knee pad strapped to his thigh, with the flight information written on it—information that he could be reviewing before his flight entered the war, because once the shooting started, he'd have to react through instinct. There wouldn't be time to review the information and try to figure out a plan of action. It would be too late.

But then, all that was something he'd done on the ground, standing in front of a huge map of North Vietnam that was twenty feet long and ten feet high. He and the other pilots had talked their way through the mission a couple of times—ingress and egress routes, targets, alternatives, evasion routes, and locations of SAR forces if that became necessary. Their route package was number one, the easiest because it was the farthest south, the farthest from Hanoi.

Now, with all that information firmly in mind, Taylor felt that there was nothing more to do. He could over-train, overstudy, and that was as bad as not being familiar with the information. Once the mission started, it was better to keep his head on a swivel, watching his instruments and the sky around him, than to study the map inside the cockpit. If there was something in the frag or the route package that he didn't know, it was too late to learn it now. He had to fly the airplane and watch for the enemy.

As they approached the coast of North Vietnam Taylor squeezed the mike button, and said, "Wasp, check."

"Two."

"Three."

"Four."

He initiated a slow descent, taking his fighters down so that the enemy radars would have a more difficult time finding and tracking them. He could use terrain masking to blind the enemy. The only problem was that at those low altitudes, ever rice farmer with a weapon shot at them. Most of the time, they missed, but a single, lucky round could kill Taylor or the pilots with him just as dead as the big triple-A batteries around Hanoi.

As he skimmed across the blue waters of the South China Sea, sweat dripping, Taylor heard the calls of other flights also moving in to attack. Taylor ignored them, concentrating on his own navigation gear and his own mission.

"Waco's got guns at one o'clock."

"Baron's got guns at one o'clock."

"Kingmen's got guns at three o'clock."

Taylor glanced at his route package information, but wasn't sure where the other flights were or even who they were. The information they were giving told him that the North Vietnamese were shooting at everyone, using the radar-guided ZSU-23/4 antiaircraft artillery. They were probably also firing their S-60s and everything else up to and including the 80-millimeter weapons. Flak would be thick, but none of it was around him. He assumed that it was farther to the north, where some lucky bastards were getting to hit important targets on the outskirts of Hanoi.

Taylor initiated a gradual turn as the rice paddies and then the jungles of North Vietnam flashed underneath his aircraft. Warning calls came from all over now. Men talking into their radios, telling each other of danger as if telling a wife to watch out for a pothole as she drove. The radio was full of the calls, full of chatter.

As the fighters raced over the ground, they crossed a rosebud pattern that had not been visible on the aerial photos the pilots had studied, nor had intelligence warned them about it. Taylor had seen pictures of it before, during intelligence briefings that had been designed to acquaint him with the enemy threat capability.

A rosebud pattern with roads between revetments. Blast shields and resupply points. They had crossed a SAM-2 site that was new, not yet operational, but one that would be, south of where it should be. They had crossed it so quickly, at such a low altitude, that Taylor barely had time to see it, but it stuck in his mind. The enemy was stepping up his defenses. It was something to give the intelligence officer during the debriefing later.

Then, suddenly, overriding everyone on the air and wiping out all other transmissions, came the call, "This is Watcher, this is Watcher, time is fifteen two—we have MiG scramble, sector November Tango. This is Watcher, out."

Taylor glanced up, outside his aircraft. Watcher had wiped out everyone's transmissions, telling them many things that no one wanted to know. The important information—the number of enemy fighters, their immediate location, their direction of flight, and the units who might be their targets—had been left out. Taylor knew that the MiG launch was far to the north of him and not directed at him because the MiGs rarely came far south, but it would have been nice to have been certain.

They reached the IP and turned inbound, the flight stringing out then. Taylor led them in, using the weather information that had been provided in Saigon. The winds, supposedly out of the north at ten knots, gusting to fifteen, made the problem of bombing difficult. Once he punched off the bombs, they were on their own, falling where they pleased. They couldn't adjust for a sudden gust of wind, if the winds were not as predicted. On the run in, Taylor had looked for signs that the weather officer had been wrong. Blowing smoke, or dust, or the leaves on the trees, could give him the information he needed, but there was nothing. He dived at the target, pickled the bombs, and began a jinking, twisting, climbing turn off the target. Flak blossomed around him, buffeting the plane. He dived and then came up, turning away from the target. He risked a glance back over his shoulder, to see the mushrooming, dark brown dirt thrown upward. There was smoke from spreading fires, and then he was busy flying the plane, watching the yellow-orange detonations around him.

He kept diving, turning, climbing, rolling, trying to confuse the enemy gunners. The black clouds of the flak batteries became fewer and fewer and then he was out again, over the South China Sea, away from North Vietnam and the enemy. Twenty minutes over hostile territory, that had seemed like a lifetime, that could have turned into the end of a lifetime. And then he was clear of the danger.

"Wasp, check."

"Two."

"Three."

"Four."

Everyone had made it in, and had made it out. There was no damage to the flight, because no one had said anything about damage. Taylor began a slow climb back to altitude, now heading toward the south, the sun beating down on him. He was completely sweat-soaked now, not all of it from the blazing sun. It was the tension of attacking a target that he had attacked before. It was the tension of flying through the enemy defenses as some unseen soldier tried to turn his multi-million-dollar airplane into a twisted, worthless wreck. Tension that came suddenly, as he crossed the coast, and disappeared almost as quickly as he escaped the north. Except that his hands shook and his breath rasped from his rapid breathing. Adrenaline was impossible to work off in a fighter cockpit. There was nowhere to run, no room to exercise as the chemical pumped through his bloodstream, turning him from a calm, professional pilot into a nervous wreck, sure that he was about to die.

He could feel the tension in his grip on the stick. He could feel it in the pit of his stomach. He could almost smell it inside the cockpit. It never failed. When the enemy started shooting, the body responded with chemicals to help it survive. Chemicals to give added strength, better sight and hearing, to help in either fighting or running. But in the aircraft, it was impossible to run or fight. He had to sit there, watching the enemy gunners, watching the flak, and listening to the radio calls of other pilots, other flights, and the adrenaline kept right on pumping.

Maybe that was where the elation came from after a bomb run. A chemical high from defying death again. Now, with the flight joined, on the way back to Saigon, Taylor wanted to sing, scream, dance, fuck, run. Anything and everything, and he could do nothing other than sit there, watching the world flash by at over six hundred miles an hour.

The radio came alive then. The fight up north suddenly turned bad. There hadn't been much in the way of SAMs used against the American fighter-bombers. Sites were still being built, but Robert McNamara and the Joint Chiefs of Staff at the Pentagon had declared them off limits. Now, suddenly, those SAM sites were operational.

"Baron, we have a single ringer."

"Baron, I have a double ringer. Just went triple."

"We have launch. Launch!"

"Breaking right and down."

"This is Watcher, at fifteen fifteen, multiple SAM launches, November Sierra, Sierra Sierra, Xray Sierra. This is Watcher, this is Watcher, out."

"Waco, I have a triple ringer."

"Waco, we have guns at ten o'clock."

"Jesus, who blew up."

"Waco, check."

"Two."

"Three."

"Waco four, do you copy?"

There was a moment of dead silence as everyone over North Vietnam waited for Waco four to answer. Then the radio exploded into chatter again as everyone tried to get the hell out. SAMs were being launched rapidly, as if the North Vietnamese had been told that if they didn't use them all they'd never get any more of them. The radio was alive with SAM warnings, calls, orders, and instructions.

And yet it all sounded relatively calm. Men telling one another what they had to know to survive. Calls of near misses and SAMs that had been tricked into diving into the rice paddies around them. As targets were hit, pilots began a rapid egress from North Vietnam, some low-leveling out, trying to avoid enemy radars. Checks were made, and it was discovered that more planes and more men had been lost to the sudden escalation in the air war.

Taylor wiped a gloved hand over his brow and took a deep breath. "Jesus," he whispered to himself and then glanced right and left, making sure that his wingman and the second element leader were tucked up close.

"Something's got to be done," said one of Taylor's pilots. "Something quick."

Taylor didn't want to tie up the air with a lot of useless chatter, not when the men still over North Vietnam needed to give each other help and instructions—but he knew the man was right. Something needed to be done.

Six hours later, dressed in the only civilian clothes that he owned in South Vietnam, William Taylor sat in a front-row seat in the Gunfighter's Club, a beer in front of him and the pilots of his flight around him. They too were dressed in civilian clothes and were guzzling beers. One of them, a young man with red hair and so many freckles that his face looked as if it had been spray-painted quickly and badly, held a glass over his head and cheered on the Vietnamese girl who was dancing in front of them. He was shouting at the top of his lungs, but no one could hear a word he was saying because of the driving beat of the rock and roll coming from a half-dozen hidden speakers that set the building to vibrating.

The Gunfighter's Club was a small, special bistro hidden on Tan Son Nhut, or rather the first idea had been to hide it, but then someone had painted giant green footprints along the road that led to the front door.

A guard sat there, keeping out the riffraff—which meant anyone who didn't have a set of wings sewn or pinned to his uniform. It made no difference if they were crew chief's wings, navigator's wings, door gunner's wings, or pilot's wings. Everyone on flight status was allowed in, and everyone not on flight status was kept out. That included generals and colonels and majors who thought they could go anywhere they pleased because of their rank.

Just inside the door was a row of lock boxes so that the helicopter pilots would have a place to store their weapons. Helicopter pilots rarely showed up unarmed. Past the lock boxes was the club proper, a huge room with a bar on one side with four men and two women working behind it. Rows and rows of bottles lined the shelves behind them, and there was a huge mirror behind that made it look as if there were twice as much liquor available as there was. In one corner was a raised stage where Vietnamese girls danced in time to music blaring from the various giant speakers. Usually it was just Vietnamese girls who danced, though sometimes American girls, guests of the pilots or crewmen, tired of the men watching the locals, would leap to the stage to compete. It made for an interesting show that sometimes degenerated into fights.

The rest of the club was filled with tables and chairs, and the chairs were filled with men in flight suits, jungle fatigues, and civilian clothes. There were only a few women in the club, because the pilots sometimes got too rowdy while they practiced carrier landings or short-field landings, using tables as the runways and beer bottles as the barricades.

Taylor picked up his beer, took a deep drink, and said, loud enough for everyone to hear, even over the music, "Those fucking wing weenies couldn't find it on a bright afternoon and using both hands."

Jack Dobbs, a young, dark-haired man with acne scars on his face, knew that Taylor was referring to the intelligence officer, the weather officer, the maintenance officer, and the operations officer, lifted his glass in salute and agreement, and took a deep drink.

The red-haired kid, named Hopper, who had been in-country for nearly two months, sat down, nodded in a long, exaggerated motion, and then nearly fell off his chair. "I agree," he said, pronouncing each word carefully.

"Christ, Hopper, how can you agree? You don't even know what the fuck was said."

Instead of answering the question, he pointed at the Vietnamese girl, who was now nearly naked. She still wore a miniature bikini bottom, but that wouldn't last very long. Her body was covered with a light coating of sweat that picked up and reflected the lights pointed at her. She had small breasts that looked hard and formed of concrete. They didn't vibrate or bounce as she danced. But she did have big nipples and they stood out, at attention.

Taylor wasn't interested in the girl, even as she rolled her bikini bottom down her thighs and kicked it free. Now completely nude, she waved her body at everyone and reached a hand down as if to finger herself.

"Fucking SAMs," said Taylor. "On the fucking restricted target list. Don't fucking destroy the fucking complexes as they're being built. Oh no, that makes too much fucking sense. Let them get operational and shoot down a couple of our boys first. Shit."

"You ever notice," said Dobbs, "that your language deteriorates in direct proportion to the number of beers you've consumed?"

"So who cares?" asked Taylor.

"No one cares," said Dobbs. He turned and waved a hand at one of the waitresses, a small girl with long black hair and a light complexion. She had large breasts that were barely concealed in the tight blouse she wore. Once in a while she would dance, ripping off her clothes as quickly as she could. But that was only once in a while.

"Everyone ready?" asked Dobbs, pointing at the almost empty beer glasses and the completely empty pitcher.

As the waitress took the pitcher, Taylor leaned forward, elbows on the table. "Someone's got to do something. Fuck, we're hanging our asses out, getting shot at, and the incompetents who stay back here can't get anything done right. Weather's always fucked up."

"You ever think," said Dobbs, "that it must be rough to predict the winds in North Vietnam without any ground reporting stations."

"Shit," said Taylor, "they get credit for a combat tour, credit for being in Vietnam, and the worst thing to happen is they catch a dose of the clap. You'd think they'd find a way to get us the information we need."

Hopper looked around the inside of the club, saw a couple of other fighter pilots and several helicopter pilots. He turned his attention back to Taylor, although out of the corner of his eye he was watching the naked woman as she danced.

Before Hopper or Dobbs could say anything, Taylor added, "And what about those pip-squeak lieutenants running BDAs. Look at a couple of pictures of the target and decide we missed. Assholes never get out of their air-conditioned bunkers but they're ready to send us back to North Vietnam so we can blow up the rubble. Don't want the North Vietnamese to get anything of value from a target that we hit yesterday and the day before that."

"Okay, Bill," said Dobbs, "that's about enough."

Taylor looked at the other man. Stared him in the eye and asked, "You like the way things are?"

Dobbs poured beer into his glass from the pitcher the waitress had just set in front of him. She had snatched the money from the table, taking enough so that she had a generous tip. Dobbs watched the head grow, the white foam filling the top of the glass and then spilling down the side. As he put the pitcher down, the naked girl fled the stage, stopping once to wiggle her bare butt, and the music died.

"No, I don't like it, but you've got to remember that there is always someone who has it rougher than you do no matter what you do."

"Right. The poor transport pilots have to fly twelve, fifteen hours a day, hauling shit from here to there, but when they reach their destination, no one's shooting at them and someone hands them a cold beer to ease their pain."

Dobbs took a deep drink and turned to Hopper. "There's no talking to him when he gets into one of these moods." He turned back to Taylor. "How'd you like to be a helicopter pilot?"

"They don't have to put up with fucking missiles, and restricted targets, and assholes in Washington who make stupid rules for us to follow."

"Okay, okay," said Dobbs. "You win."

Taylor slapped the table and stared at the other pilot. "It's just that you don't see the whole picture. You see only part of it. There is no fucking reason for us to have to put up with this shit over the targets. If it wasn't for the candy asses in the Pentagon and Congress who are afraid of fighting a war, we wouldn't have to hang our butts out. They talk of a limited war and a measured response. What's that get you? Dead pilots and broken machines."

The music came up again and a fully dressed Vietnamese girl danced out to center stage. She stood there, swaying in time to music that only she heard. Slowly, she began to move around, pulling at the long zipper that ran from the hem of her short skirt all the way to the collar.

Taylor ignored her, too. He studied Dobbs and then Hopper. "You like flying through all that shit? You like the idea of missiles coming at you?"

Dobbs didn't answer, but Hopper did. "No. Of course I don't."

"There you have it then. Someone had better come up with a way to suppress the fucking SAMs or a lot of good men are going to die. And they better come up with it in one hell of a fucking hurry."

"They will," said Dobbs, not knowing how right he was. He pointed to the girl, who had dropped her dress and was dancing in only her tiny panties and almost invisible bra. "Now, let's just watch the show."

Taylor picked up his beer and drained it. He stood up, stared directly into the brown eyes of the dancing girl, and shook his head. To Dobbs he said, "I'm heading on back. Want to catch some sleep so that I'll be ready when they decide that only I can win the war by dying in the north."

Dobbs raised his glass in a mock salute. "The rest of us appreciate your dedication and devotion to duty. You truly are a warrior."

"Fuck you very much," said Taylor. He headed for the door.

# TWO

THERE were only a few people sitting in the first couple of rows in the large theaterlike auditorium. The raised stage in front of the screen contained an American flag on one side and the California state flag on the other. There was a podium set forward, on one corner of the stage. Only the lights directly over the stage were turned on, but it was still fairly bright in the auditorium.

Military officers, pilots and electronic warfare officers, wondering why they had been summoned there on such short notice, were waiting less patiently. They occupied the first couple of rows in the theater, and there was a single MP standing near the doors at the rear of the place. No one seemed to know anything, except that the meeting, briefing, or lecture would start in a few minutes.

Major Paul Osborne sat there quietly, reading a paperback novel. Osborne was a tall man with sandy hair, blue eyes, and a pointed, narrow nose. He had a mustache that was just outside of the regulation grooming standard, but no one seemed to care about that. He was a quiet man who had been in the Air Force long enough to know that the briefing wouldn't start on time and that he could finish a couple of chapters of his book.

Osborne had come up through the ranks, enlisting in the Air Force right out of high school, thinking that he could become a pilot. Then he had learned about the college requirements for both officer candidate school and flight school. The first chance he got, about a year after he enlisted, he started attending night classes. With a waiver in hand, he was allowed to attend college full-time, the Air Force picking up some of the expenses, on the promise that he'd reenter the Air Force for five years. It seemed like a good deal and he had taken it.

Now, after all that, including various flight schools, he sat in a room with only a couple of men he knew by sight. They were sitting together, talking quietly. The rest of the men were waiting impatiently for someone to get the show on the road. That was the way it was in the Air Force—you were thrown into situations with men you'd seen around but didn't know, and told to hurry up because it was important that everything get started on time. And then you waited because someone else, somewhere else, had dropped the ball.

Finally a side door opened and a colonel moved to the stage. He stopped in front of the podium, snapped on the small light above it, and placed a folder on the podium's surface. He turned, glanced at the screen, and saw the first slide pop into place—a bright-red thing designed to attract attention to it.

It was just like the Air Force, thought Osborne. Lots of good pictures to go along with the briefing. Never tell a man anything when you couldn't show him a couple of pictures of it at the same time to reinforce the message. For the conclusion of the briefing, they would tell him what they had just told him, in case he wasn't listening the first time.

As Osborne closed his book and the others in the room fell silent, the colonel at the lectern leaned into the microphone. "Good morning, gentlemen," he said, his voice booming through the auditorium as the speakers squealed with feedback.

When the noise had faded, the colonel said more quietly, "I'm Colonel Lukenbach, and I'll be conducting this portion of the briefing. Please remember that everything discussed in this room is classified secret and will not be discussed with anyone not cleared to hear it or in a facility that is not adequately protected."

He reached over, pushed a button, and the lights went out. The slide, which had reinforced the secret nature of the briefing, was replaced with another that looked cobbled together by someone with little artistic talent.

"Code name of the project is Ferret, because we intend to ferret out the enemy's missile and triple-A defenses to destroy them."

There was no reaction to that, and the slide changed again. "In the last forty-eight hours, the enemy, that is, the North Vietnamese Army, has begun using a SAM system developed in the Soviet Union. First intelligence pictures of this system were taken during the 1957 May

Day Parade through Red Square. We didn't know its function at that time, but we've since received more and better intelligence."

The picture changed to one of a missile, thirty or forty feet long, carried on the back of a truck. There were rows of them, all in line, as they drove through the wide, wet streets of Moscow.

"Background of the weapon is varied and interesting. It is believed that this system, named Guideline by NATO, is a multistage antiaircraft missile, radar guided, and that it was used to shoot down Gary Powers in 1960. The Soviet claim at the time was that they had used a new missile, and the subsequent information has suggested that the SA-2 has the necessary slant range to accomplish the task. It was also used during the Cuban missile crisis and destroyed the high-flying U-2 piloted by Major Rudolph Anderson. Major Anderson was killed during that recon mission."

Again the slide changed. There was an aerial photograph of a rosebud-shaped complex. There were roads between the petals of the bud, and the launch equipment was displayed, as was a configuration for the various support vans and vehicles.

"These areas," said Lukenbach, as he turned and pointed at the screen, "have been erected recently in North Vietnam, first around the Hanoi and then Haiphong areas, and then spreading out farther to the south, to defend other points of strategic significance. These sites are typical of the SA-2 Guideline sites built in the Soviet Union and in Cuba.

"It was not until recently that any of the sites were operational. No missiles had been seen in the launch areas, no radar and other support vehicles had been seen, and there was no crew to use the system. That is, until two days ago. Then the enemy began launching missiles at our bombing missions."

No one in the audience said a word. Lukenbach looked down at them, waiting. When no one spoke, he continued. "We have retaliated against each of the sites that launched missiles at our fighters and bombers, but we don't want to get into a war of attrition, trading pilots and fighters for SAMs and sites . . ."

One of the men stood up and said, "I got a question. We know beforehand what those sites were for?"

"If you mean, did we know they were missile complexes before the first missiles were brought in and launched, the answer is yes. The shape is distinctive—a rosebud pattern with service roads to each of the six launch areas. There is no question of what the site was going to become."

"Then why in the hell did we wait for the North Vietnamese to get them built and operational before we attacked them?" There was anger in that voice.

Lukenbach clasped his hands together and leaned on the lectern, staring at the dark shape of the questioner. "That is the policy as dictated by the Secretary of Defense. Orders were not to attack any missile site until it fired at us. Orders are not to attack MiG fighters encountered over North Vietnam unless they fire first. Orders are not to interdict enemy fighters sitting on the ground until those fighters are airborne and have attacked us."

"Shit, sir, that is a damned stupid policy." The man dropped back into his seat to a burst of applause.

Lukenbach stared down at the officer for a moment and then shook his head. "We're not here to discuss the policy as established by the Secretary of Defense, the Chiefs of Staff, or other members of the administration . . ."

"No, sir," said the man. "But it's what happens when you hire some corporate weenie to head a department where he has no expertise."

Lukenbach grinned to himself but said, "Let's not get embroiled in a debate about the relative merits of various civilians who hold positions of power in the civilian end of the chain of command. Right now our major concern is the SAMs being used against our strike forces in North Vietnam."

The picture changed to one of an F-100F Super Sabre sitting on a ramp. There was a dung-colored hangar in the background along with such a beautiful formation of clouds that the picture had to be faked.

Lukenbach turned, studied the picture for a moment, and then said, "The solution to the problem is one that has been discussed in secret meetings for some time. Proposals have been made and then rejected because there has been no observable need for the system."

Lukenbach leaned on the podium and said, in a voice tinged with awe, "Gentlemen, with the introduction of a few pieces of electronic gear, and the addition of a couple of antennae, these aircraft can be modified into SAM killers."

Lukenbach went on to explain what modifications were anticipated and then into the theoretical tactics that the new fighters would employ. He talked about SAM suppression as opposed to site destruction and talked about the effects of that suppression. He mentioned that the SAMs could limit the effectiveness of the air war if something wasn't done to stop them. A counter weapon had to be developed, and although earlier suggestions and theories had been dismissed as unimportant and of no use, that decision had been suddenly reversed—by surface-to-air missiles exploding under American aircraft.

It went on that way for another thirty minutes, with Lukenbach running through all the slides that he had brought with him. They included the May Day pictures of the SA-2 and more aerial shots of the launch complexes, with the missiles sitting there waiting. When he finished with everything he wanted to say, he asked, "Are there any questions?"

Osborne raised hs hand and asked, "When is all this supposed to be operational? Meaning, how soon does the Pentagon expect us to be ready to fight back?"

"Realistically? I'd say three to six months, but you know the Air Force. Everything was supposed to be finished early last week."

As soon as his briefing in Saigon was finished, Major Taylor didn't know whether to cheer or curse. Finally, the assholes in Washington had released the SAM sites from the restricted-targets list. That could be viewed from two points of view. One was that now they got to attack the enemy, and the other was that they would have to attack the enemy. It was all a matter of perspective. Taylor was one of the few who didn't particularly like the idea.

After the briefing he stood outside the briefing room,

under the hot, tropical sun, sweat staining his flight suit, and watched as the other pilots came boiling out of the building. They were laughing, joking, slapping each other on the back, and ignoring the upcoming mission.

Taylor seized Dobbs and said, "You understand what this all means?"

Dobbs frowned and squinted in the sun. Slowly he pulled a pair of sunglasses from his pocket and put them on. "It means we're going to get a chance to get even with those silly bastards up north."

"It means, idiot, that we're going to attack SAM sites that can shoot back. They're going to launch two-ton missiles, each one holding damned near three hundred pounds of high explosives, to try to blow us out of the sky. They don't have to hit us. Close is good enough."

"You're never happy," said Dobbs.

Taylor wiped the sweat from his face. "I'm never happy because I have to put up with bullshit. We should have taken those targets out weeks ago. Everyone knew what they were going to be."

"Well, now we've got the chance."

"Right, with them armed and waiting. You know that it's not only the missiles. They'll have the 23- and 57-millimeter weapons ready for us. They'll be throwing up a cloud of steel."

Dobbs shrugged and asked, "What would you do differently?"

Now Taylor smiled. "You don't want to get me started." He began walking toward the personal-equipment room and then turned so that he could talk to Dobbs. "First, I'd take off the stupid restrictions. You going to fight a war, you fight a war. You don't limit your side with stupid restrictions. If you're not prepared to fight a war, a full-scale, hell-bent-for-leather war, a kill-everyone-in-sight-and-don't-take-any-prisoners war, then you don't get involved."

They began walking toward the equipment room again. "There may be things that we don't understand," said Dobbs. "Political reasons for the restrictions."

Taylor nodded and said, "Which is my point. If there are such reasons, then you shouldn't be fighting the war in the first place. You'd have thought that we'd have learned that lesson in Korea. You can't limit your partic-ipation in the war when the enemy is doing everything he can to win."

They reached the personal-equipment room. It was in a small, air-conditioned building near the flight line. All the gear they would need for the upcoming mission was stored and carefully checked inside the building. It was the place where the pilots got ready to actually go out and fly the airplanes. It was like the locker room used by football players before their game.

Taylor got the door and Dobbs entered. He stopped then and said, "You don't really believe that, do you? Believe everything you just said?"

"What? That we either fight the war or we don't? What's not to believe? It's a simple fact. If you are not prepared to do everything possible to win, then you have no right committing men to that war. It's like tell-ing a football team they can do everything they want to move the ball, until they get to the twenty yard line. Then they have to surrender it to the other side."

"That's stupid."

"Of course," said Taylor, "and no one is getting killed in the football game."

They moved to their lockers and opened them. Taylor began to get rid of everything that was personal. Wallet, rings, unit patches, and the like. The theory was, if you were shot down and captured, you would be carrying nothing that the enemy could use. Unit insignia could tell the enemy where you were stationed and might give him clues about the unit. No one wanted to make the job of the enemy easier.

Taylor, like the others, was dressed in a one-piece cotton flying suit, a design that made life miserable in the tropics. Although he hadn't seen many Army pilots wearing them, he knew that the Army had a two-piece flight suit that allowed the air to circulate and cool the body.

He struggled into his G suit. It looked like chaps with zippers and could be used as a flotation device if he went down in the water. It was covered with pockets full of survival gear. Almost everyone knew that the first thing a downed pilot did was run away from his airplane leaving everything behind that wasn't somehow fastened to his body. That was why there were all the pockets filled with the things a pilot needed to survive on the ground.

Dobbs had sat down on the long bench between the lockers and was getting into his mesh survival vest. It contained more gear, including a holster for a pistol and loops for extra ammunition. Some of the pilots preferred to wear a gunbelt like the cowboys of the Old West because it held more ammo and they claimed that it sort of balanced everything out.

Taylor pulled out his vest and checked the water bottles. Again, studies had shown that almost everyone who went down had an uncontrollable thirst. They would risk their lives for a drink of water.

Taylor sat down next to Dobbs, who looked up at him, his face suddenly strangely pale. "I don't think I'm coming back from this one."

"Christ, Dobbs," said Taylor, "what kind of bullshit are you handing out now?"

"It's a feeling." Dobbs shook his head as sweat beaded on his forehead. "Oh, shit, I knew it." He was angry now, as well as frightened. He glanced up at Taylor and added, "We've been getting away with too much for too long. It's bound to catch up with us. Catch up with me."

Taylor shook his head in disgust. "I've heard this before. Hell, it's a cliché in every war movie ever made. Guy has a premonition that he's going to get killed, writes good-bye letters to everyone he knows, and goes out to get zapped just as he knew he would."

"Yeah . . ."

"Listen, I've talked to a dozen guys who've felt that way. Hell, I felt that way myself. I was suddenly sure that I was going to get killed. Absolutely knew it. The trick is to not make it into a self-fulfilling prophecy. Instead of being reckless because you're going to die anyway, you have to be more careful so that you don't get killed. Be more alert."

"I wish I could stand down on this one."

Taylor raised an eyebrow and asked, "You serious?"

"I don't know." Dobbs rubbed his face with both

hands. His color was still bad. "If someone else takes my place and gets killed, I'd feel . . ."

"Look," said Taylor, standing up, "if you really want out of this mission, I can get someone to take your place, but you're better off flying it. You can't let these ridiculous feelings get to you. Too much important shit to do."

Dobbs sat there quietly for a moment, listening to the noise around them. Other pilots were getting ready to go out and attack the SAM sites, others to go out on other missions. They were laughing and joking and one man was telling several others about the night he'd spent on Tu Do Street with a French-Vietnamese whore who could and would do anything for a price.

"There was nothing she wouldn't try," the man announced to all who would listen.

Finally Dobbs looked up and said, "I'll fly it." It's not fair to dump my responsibilities on someone else."

Taylor slapped him on the shoulder and said, "And if you get killed, I'll buy the first round at the Gunfighter's Club tonight."

Although everything was secret, top secret, and as secret as it could get, there was a staff car waiting for Osborne when he finished learning about the SAM-suppression problem over North Vietnam. Some of the men were detailed into training facilities on the base, into map rooms, and into secret briefings to discuss the air defenses generally, and the SA-2 Guideline SAM specifically.

Lukenbach took Osborne outside, down the stairs, and into the waiting staff car. The tech sergeant who was the driver closed the back doors and then slipped behind the wheel. He didn't wait for instructions. He dropped the car into gear and pulled away from the entrance of the building. Osborne didn't ask any questions, figuring that he would get all the answers later. Besides, the car was air-conditioned and comfortable and he didn't have to drive.

They left the base, slowing just long enough for the guards to wave them through. They got up on the freeway, where the driver attempted to keep up with the flow of traffic and avoid running into any of the other cars, which seemed to want to create burning, smoking wreckage.

After ten minutes, Lukenbach turned and said, "We'll be touring the facility where the special modifications will be made."

Osborne nodded toward the driver.

"Sergeant Masterson is fully cleared and does not talk out of school, do you, sergeant?"

"No, sir."

"Just what modifications are being made?" asked Osborne.

"What we want to do is take an operational F-100, gut it of the nonessential wiring and gear, and then add our new equipment. You'll get equipment that will spot the SAM sites and the radar facilities and pinpoint them for you. Once they begin to search for you, you'll know and be in a position to stop them."

"Okay," said Osborne, unsure of what to say. He kept his eyes on the freeway, and the landscape that he could see from the car. He wasn't exactly sure what he'd gotten himself into and was wondering if it was too late to get himself out of it.

"Intel came up with something else. We've got the frequencies that the enemy Fan Song radars use while in the search mode, and we've learned that just before a launch, there is a sudden boost in the signal. That means we can put a launch-detection warning light in the cockpit of every plane over North Vietnam."

They slid to the left, toward an exit, and then down the ramp. They turned left, joining the traffic along a busy street. As they stopped for a red light, the sergeant turned, an arm on the back of his seat.

"Sir, once we get inside the long Beach complex, security is going to be tight. Civilian guards will probably want to see some ID before you're allowed to roam around."

When the light changed, they started again. At the entrance to the Long Beach plant, they stopped and each man showed his ID card. The guard consulted a list and said, "I don't see Major Osborne's name."

"Of course not," said Lukenbach. "He wasn't selected until this morning. I'll vouch for him."

The guard shoved a clipboard into the open car window. "You've got to sign."

Lukenbach scribbled his name on the sheet, wrote in Osborne's, and handed the clipboard back. The guard, happy with that, waved them through.

"We're going directly to the hangar where the plane is being housed."

A few moment later they stopped in front of a huge hangar painted desert tan. There was a brick building attached to the front that looked as if it had been added as an afterthought. The glass windows, tinted a dark green like giant sunglass lenses, looked out on the airfield.

The sergeant got out and opened the rear doors for Lukenbach and Osborne. While the sergeant remained behind, Lukenbach took Osborne to the closest door, in the building. Before they could get there, it opened, and a civilian, dressed in a white, short-sleeve shirt, tie, and wrinkled gray pants stepped out.

"Welcome, Colonel."

Lukenbach nodded and gestured toward Osborne. "Major Osborne, this is John Pip, who is in charge of the project here. John, this is Major Paul Osborne."

"Major," said Pip, holding out a hand.

Osborne noticed that the man had a pocket protector in his shirt, filled with pens and pencils. There were stains on the shirt, one looking like coffee and the other like egg yolk. He also noticed that the man looked tired, as if he had been working day and night to get everything ready.

Pip let both pass him to enter first and then hurried around them, leading them down a short hall. He reached a door with a fire bar handle on it and stood there for a moment before opening it.

"You both know that this project is classified." He laughed and added, "It's so secret that the tech rep wasn't even told about it. Don't want to tip our hands."

Osborne was about to say something to that but then remembered just how many projects had been compromised because no one thought them important enough to really safeguard.

"If you're ready?"

Lukenbach nodded and Pip pushed open the door. The hangar was huge and the whole floor had been waxed until it was a dull brown color. There were black marks on the floor from aircraft tires, but now it was empty except for a single F-100 standing near the gigantic doors. The sleek, silver plane didn't look different than any of the hundreds of others that Osborne had seen. He took a step toward it and read the tail number: 58-1231.

"If you'll come with me," said Pip, "I'll show you exactly what we've done to improve the aircraft and to ready it for the mission."

Osborne wasn't sure that he wanted to see every little modification, but didn't say a word. He followed the engineer into the hangar and across the waxed floor. His footsteps echoed hollowly as he walked because there was nothing else in the hangar, except a yellow tug that would pull the aircraft out into the sunlight, if someone wanted a test flight.

Pip stood at the nose of the aircraft and said, "We've had to add a couple of external antennae, and we've picked up a buffeting in the aircraft. Nothing big, and we're working to redesign the antennae or the placement to dampen out the buffeting."

Osborne nodded and asked, "Will this really give us a way to defeat the SAMs?"

"Locates them for you. Tells you that the radar is operating and where the site is. That means you can attack them."

Lukenbach glanced at Pip and added, "This next bit is confidential. I don't want to hear either of you mentioning it again, but the Navy is working on a missile that will ride the radar beam back to the site and destroy the van."

Osborne had to grin. "And without the radar, the enemy is blind. Unable to launch."

"Exactly."

"I love it," said Osborne.

# THREE

T HE weather turned to shit just after takeoff. They had lifted into a beautiful, cloudless blue sky, but before they had flown more than a hundred miles, they could see the flat gray line of a front coming just as the weather weenie had said it would. It had been predicted by the weather weenie, but he had been wrong so often that Taylor had hoped they wouldn't hit the front.

As they approached it, he elected to pop up over it, flying on top of the cloud deck. He stayed in the bright sunlight, the clouds spread out under him like a lumpy blanket waiting for the picnickers. A dirty, gray blanket.

With only the roar of the engine to keep him company, along with the dancing needles on the instruments, he let his mind roam. There was a peacefulness to flying above the clouds like this. Glancing right or left he could see his wingman or the airplanes of the flight's other element, but by concentrating on what lay ahead, he could block them out. He was the only person alive in a world designed just for his pleasure. A quiet world with only weather and fuel limitations as the enemy.

Occasionally, in the distance, he could see other aircraft. Transport planes painted in strange camouflage patterns, commercial jets with loads of FNGs to be thrown into the war, other fighters, and sometimes helicopters when their pilots had nothing better to do than clutter the sky with their inferior machines.

He let his eyes drop to the Doppler navigation system that had been preprogrammed with the flight route. Without ground reference, he had to rely on it. The system worked well, most of the time. It only failed at critical moments when he was the flight leader. Then navigational duties devolved to the second element leader. But, at the moment, the system was operating well, and he didn't have a care in the world.

Except for the SAM sites in North Vietnam. That thought came up at him with the speed of a Guideline. He put it out of his mind, trying to enjoy the serenity of the flight, and his thoughts of the whores in Saigon— the ones who danced nightly in the Gunfighter's Club and who would, if they happened to like you, take you back to their houses or apartments and dance for you in private.

Taylor grinned to himself and tried to roll his shoulders, but with all the equipment he was required to wear and with the shoulder harness and seat belt, it was difficult to move anything other than his hands and feet on the controls. He was strapped in a flying coffin, traveling through the air at over six hundred miles an hour.

Not a coffin, he told himself, almost shouting the words out loud. Sometimes he talked to himself, just to hear a real, human voice and not the tinny, static-masked voices of the other pilots and the ground controllers.

The girl last night, he thought. She'd been a beauty. Black hair to her waist, long, tanned legs, and high, pointed breasts. A girl that could make your heart stop with her smile and who could knock you dead with a small kindness. A girl who had shed her clothes slowly, making everyone in the Gunfighter's Club ache with anticipation.

It was a pleasant thought and then it was interrupted. He glanced at the clock and then the Doppler, and realized that it was time to rendezvous with the tankers. He turned toward the east, his eyes searching the unbroken sky, and could see nothing of the KC-135. Taylor made a call, and the response from the tanker sounded like it was coming from a long distance, maybe the other side of the world.

"Say again," said Taylor.

The tanker radars had picked him up and the operator gave him the vector. Taylor rogered, and turned to the northeast. Two minutes later a flash of sunlight off the metal of the tanker pinpointed the aircraft for him.

"I have you in sight," said Taylor. "Flight of four needing full fuel."

"Roger."

Taylor turned again, a shallow bank to the left until he was behind the tanker and just below it. While the bigger plane flew along slowly, straight and level, its boom extended, Taylor tried to slip up on it carefully, just nudging the throttles and using his airspeed and his attitude as he approached, adjusting himself so that his velocity matched that of the KC-135. Over the radio, the boom operator tried to help with contradictory instructions that Taylor chose to ignore as he stared at the boom hanging from the rear of the jet tanker aircraft.

He made contact and watched as the fuel gauges that had been dropping began to climb again. When he had a full fuel load, he radioed the information and then broke away. The flight stayed with the tanker until each aircraft had been refueled. They all broke away, turned to the left, and began heading toward North Vietnam.

"Thanks for the gas," said Taylor, as he pushed the throttle and wound it up to full RPM.

But he couldn't slip back into a calm frame of mind, boring holes in the sky as he flew over the South China Sea. They were too close to North Vietnam now. He had to clear all the nonsense, all the bullshit, from his mind and concentrate on the mission.

As he turned to the left, toward the northwest, still on top of the cloud deck, he said, "Wasp, check."

"Two."

"Three."

"Four."

Everyone was still with him. He glanced out of the cockpit, at the sky in front of him. There were no breaks in the clouds, just as the weather weenie had suggested. But the man had also put the bottom at nine thousand feet. There was supposed to be a solid undercast, and then a layer of broken clouds. Plenty of room to operate and without anything to give the enemy gunners an extra advantage. The broken clouds could help hide his flight.

"Beginning gradual let down."

Now everything that had happened to him in his life, everything that he had seen and done, was gone. All that he knew was the flying of his machine and the mission at hand. All his experiences in flight school, in training, and in flying in the war came to him. Everything that he knew that could save his life was ready for him, if he needed it.

The flight slipped into the clouds, and the formation spread out as the pilots flipped on their nav lights. Once they broke out, the lights would be extinguished. The gray wrapped Taylor and seemed to strike the aircraft with a solid force. He bounced as the winds in the clouds caught him and swirled around him. Water hit the canopy and slid back rapidly, caught in the slipstream. The instruments in front of him seemed to be the only thing left in a world that had gone mad.

And then there was a flash of deep green and he was out of the clouds. North Vietnam was now visible.

"Wasp, check."

"Two."

"Three."

"Four."

The flight was joined. He glanced at his map, at the Doppler, and then at the ground, looking for a railroad and highway near a river. Both the highway and the railroad bowed toward the river. He spotted it in front of him and knew that the nav system was working just as it should be.

"Wasp flight, let's get rid of the tanks."

The centerline, external fuel tanks dropped away, tumbling toward the ground, looking like napalm canisters dropped by close air support jets.

"Let's clean it up and get ready."

"Wasp, weak guns at three o'clock."

"Wasp, weak guns at eight o'clock, low."

Taylor glanced to the left, over his shoulder. Beyond the aircraft there, he could see a string of tracers climb and then disappear into cloud. Nothing to be concerned about.

There was a single, yellow-orange puff and then a black cloud burst in front of him. Flak from either a 37- or a 57-millimeter. Nothing to worry about there either. Yet.

"Flak to the left."

"No joy." Taylor hadn't seen it.

Taylor heard a buzzing in his headset that sounded like the biggest, meanest rattlesnake in history.

"Strong guns."

As he warned the others, the sky around him exploded. Flak bursts. Angry, red-orange fire and then black, fluffy clouds that looked almost friendly. Shrapnel bounced off the plane and Taylor ducked instinctively.

"Taking it down," he said.

He started a rapid descent, diving from under the base of the clouds, winding through the broken overcast, using it to disguise his course until he was close to the ground, then using the terrain to hide him from the enemy. He roared over the landscape at low level, his engine sucking the fuel from his tanks like a hungry monster.

In front of him he could see the buildings, the mud hootches, with their tin roofs flashing in the stray sunlight that managed to penetrate the overcast. People were scattering, running from their homes as if afraid they were the targets. A single farmer stood knee-deep in a rice paddy, an AK-47 pointed at the planes. He was firing on full auto, hosing down the sky. Taylor laughed because he had no idea where the bullets were going and suspected the farmer was equally ignorant.

Then, in front of him, at the extreme range of his vision, he saw the SAM site—an angry, ugly scar on the deep green of North Vietnam. Slight embankments rose around each launch site so that one bomb wouldn't destroy all the missiles and the whole complex. As they approached, Taylor could see the missiles lying in wait. Six telephone-pole-sized and -shaped objects, waiting, waiting, waiting.

"Guns at twelve o'clock."

Taylor wasn't sure if that was meant for him or some other flight leader. There were now other flights in other areas, and other pilots making calls.

"SAM launch. *SAM launch!*"

As Taylor watched one of the SAMs leaped from the ground in front of him, in a blast of fire and flame and a swirling cloud of dust and smoke. It came off the launcher slowly, twisting toward his flight, coming right at him.

Taylor pushed the stick and dived for the ground. He turned and twisted, just as the missile did, turning toward it and then away from, jinking right and left in a wild series of maneuvers as the flight fought to stay close to him.

The SAM lifted toward the sky, turned toward the flight, and then seemed blinded. It began a climb, then turned again and dived into the ground. There was an explosion—a geyser of mud and water and a burst of flame.

"Guns, guns, guns!"

The call meant nothing. Taylor could see the defensive systems of the missile site open up. Tracers arced toward the flight. Glowing red and green balls. Those coming directly at him seemed larger, more deadly. Taylor began a slow descent, letting the enemy gunners fire over the top of his flight.

"SAM launch."

Taylor had no idea who was talking now. He'd seen nothing from the complex in front of him. As the call was made, he dived, then began a rapid climb, trying to gain altitude so that he could attack the enemy site.

As soon as he had what looked like the right picture, he dived, opening fire with his cannon. Rounds slammed into the ground, tearing at the turf, the embankments, and the missiles. There was a secondary explosion and fire blossomed. One missile seemed to launch, climbed forty or fifty feet, and then dived into the ground, sticking in the soft mud of a rice paddy. Smoke billowed, obscuring the complex.

Behind him, his wingman attacked, using his air-to-ground rockets. The radar vans exploded. Men dived from other vehicles, running for cover. Infantry soldiers crouched there, firing upward with everything they had, and .51-caliber machine guns dotted around the site opened fire, their tracers looking miniature compared to those of the bigger weapons.

Then they were past the missile complex, streaking away from it. Taylor shot a glance to the rear but could tell nothing.

"How'd it look?"

"On fire, missiles destroyed."

*"SAM launch!"*

Taylor took immediate evasive action. He turned right and then left, climbing upward and jerking the aircraft around. The ruined missile site appeared in front of him again, several columns of jet-black smoke hiding much of it.

He broke in one direction and the second element broke in the other. He saw a missile come up out of nowhere, a gigantic thing that aimed itself at the other two aircraft. The element leader broke down and away as the missile turned and detonated. The fiery cloud engulfed the second aircraft, lifting it. The nose dropped slowly as it began to turn over. The canopy blew off as if the pilot was trying to get out. Fire spread along the fuselage. Black smoke trailed from the aircraft as it continued to rotate until it was upside down.

Over the radio came, "Get out. Get out! *Get out!*"

But the pilot didn't eject. The plane righted itself, the flames all over it, blowing back, away from the nose. If the pilot was going to bail out, it was time. But still there was no explosion from the ejection seat, no sudden blossoming of a parachute canopy.

*"Get out!"*

And then the plane blew up. A giant flash of fire and flame, a rolling, expanding cloud of smoke and fire as the jet disintegrated.

"Jesus!"

Taylor felt like he had just run a mile and then been punched in the gut. Out of breath. His chest hurt and he had to think to breathe. He turned, diving toward the ground. Around him the enemy gunners continued to fire.

The radio was alive with chatter, not only from his own flight now. Others were attacking the SAM sites. Men shouted warnings, launch detections, gun locations. Orders were given. Planes dived, climbed, and attacked. The ground winked and flashed under the assault. All of it was transmitted over the radio as Taylor tried to get his flight organized.

A second SAM site appeared in front of them and Taylor dived on it, using everything he had left. He screamed down on it, yelling to himself in the cockpit as he flipped the switches arming his weapons systems. He squeezed off the rockets, watching the tails flame, putting out a trail of white smoke. There were explosions in front of him. Geysers of dirt as the weapons hit, ripping up the enemy emplacements.

Then the flight was beyond that, climbing into the sky, toward the safety of the cloud deck. Tracers from enemy gunners followed them. Glowing red balls, chasing them. Taylor dodged around, making it harder for the enemy.

And then he was into the safety of the clouds, surrounded by the grayness of oblivion. And just as suddenly, he was out of it, into the brightness of the sun-soaked sky. He leveled off, turned, his eyes open, looking for MiGs, not sure that the enemy would be waiting for him.

Convinced that he was all alone on top of the slate-gray clouds, he turned toward the safety of the south. As he did, he said, "Wasp, check."

"Two."

"Three."

And then silence.

He had been sure that number four had exploded, and there was no indication that the pilot had gotten out. But at six hundred knots, things sometimes got overlooked. Strange things happened to pilots and planes.

"Wasp four, do you copy?"

Again the silence. No beeper from the survival radio. No parachute seen before the plane exploded. Absolutely nothing. Wasp four was gone.

Taylor felt the urge to say something, but didn't know what it would be. There was no sense staying on station to organize a rescue because there was no one to rescue. The mission was now to get back to Saigon with the last three aircraft.

Still, he felt that he was running out on a friend. The Marines sometimes sacrificed the living to recover the dead, but that was a different situation. They were on the ground, near their friends who had died. They had the chance to get the bodies back . . . but Taylor had no chance. Wasp four was gone. Blown into tiny pieces that a thorough search would probably miss if there was any way for him to search for the plane and pilot. There was nothing for him to do except to get out with the rest of the flight.

All around him the war was still going on. The radio was full of others still in the flight—calls of guns firing and SAMs launching—but they were the follow-on missions, programmed from other bases, hitting other targets. There was nothing for Taylor to do or to say. He didn't want to tie up the radio with a lot of unnecessary chatter. People died when pilots started talking unnecessarily on the radio.

He pushed the aircraft faster then, racing toward the safety of the coastline. He kept his eyes moving and his ears open, but the MiGs apparently stayed on the ground. No one had reported any enemy fighters.

They reached the coast a few minutes later and turned toward the south, keeping the enemy territory off their right wings, ten, twelve miles away. Taylor scanned his instruments again and again and kept his eyes combing the skies around them, but the enemy hadn't launched any fighters.

Again they rendezvoused with the tanker, each aircraft taking on more fuel. That finished, they turned to the south and Saigon. Unlike the trip north, Taylor didn't find his mind wandering to naked whores dancing for his pleasure or thoughts of nights spent in downtown Saigon. Instead he found himself thinking about the young lieutenant who had been flying as Wasp four. Only a few months in-country, with a little experience in fighters, he had wanted nothing more than to be a fighter pilot. He had tried hard to gain their respect, doing his job with the professionalism that was demanded by everyone else.

Lieutenant David Calhoun had tried to be the best he could, listening to the old hands and volunteering when no one else did. He had tried very hard to be one of the boys, but there had been something about him. A mannerism or the slightness of his body had made him the target of practical jokes. He had pretended that they didn't bother him, and yet Taylor knew that every joke had hurt him.

Now it was too late to do anything about it. He had had the bad luck to fly into the surface-to-air missile. The greatest pilot who ever lived wouldn't have been able to do anything in the same circumstances.

Taylor told himself over and over that there was no reason to launch the SAR forces. No reason to endanger those men when it was obvious that Calhoun had not lived to get out of the plane. The SAR forces, old A1-E Skyraiders and HH-53 helicopters, did an amazing job. Taylor had been surprised to learn that they managed to get about eighty percent of the men out of North Vietnam when it was known that the pilots had reached the ground alive.

But that did Calhoun no good. Taylor knew that. Knew it deep in his heart, and yet he still felt that he had let Calhoun down in some unexplained and unexplainable fashion.

The flight back to Saigon seemed to take forever. Taylor watched his instruments, knew that they were eating up the ground at six hundred knots, yet everything seemed to move in slow motion. The needles on the instruments seemed to be frozen, and the Doppler seemed to have broken. Progress was measured so slowly that Taylor was almost convinced they had run into some kind of a monster head wind that was holding them stationary over the ground.

But then, almost suddenly, they were in the landing pattern at Tan Son Nhut, flying around the edge of Saigon and approaching the airfield from the south. They landed on the active runway, and taxied to the revetment area. As Taylor finally shut down his engine, a jeep roared up. As he raised the canopy so that he could get out, and the hot, moist air of the tropics could get in, he saw that the squadron commander was sitting there, waiting for him.

Taylor pulled off his helmet as the crew chief set the ladder next to the fuselage. He climbed up and took Taylor's helmet from his hand.

"Welcome back, sir."

Taylor looked up at him. He knew that the crew chief knew they had left one in North Vietnam. Everyone would be counting airplanes as they landed at Tan Son Nhut and realize that one was missing. And Taylor's radio message to operations had told them who it was.

Taylor unbuckled his seat belt and tossed the shoulder harnass back over his head. The crew chief held out a hand and helped Taylor stand up. As Taylor climbed down the ladder, the jeep crawled forward and stopped close to him.

"Need to see you in my office as soon as you've finished the intel debriefing."

"There was nothing I could do."

"I understand that, but I've got some paperwork to fill out and we've got to make the notification of the next of kin."

Taylor took a deep breath and wiped the sweat from his face. "He was killed. There's no doubt about that."

"Fine," said the colonel. "I'll meet with you in about thirty minutes." He nodded at the driver and they roared off the airfield.

"Got some combat damage here, sir," said the crew

chief, pointing to the wings. There were small holes in the upper surfaces, looking like rips. "Shrapnel."

"No big thing," said Taylor. He was suddenly very tired and he didn't know why. Most of the time he was ready to go drink and have a good time after a mission, but this time was different. He just wanted to head back to his hootch and sleep. He wasn't interested in a cold beer at the Gunfighter's Club. He wasn't interested in much of anything. Without another word to the crew chief he walked off the field, ignoring the smell of jet fuel and the heat of the afternoon.

# FOUR

P AUL Osborne watched as the F-100 was wheeled
out into the sunlight. He watched as the "Remove
Before Flight" flags were pulled off, and then
waited as a pilot strolled out toward the aircraft. He
waited quietly, wondering why he had been brought out
there.

Finally Lukenbach turned and said, "We'd like you to
ride in the back for an orientation flight. The test pilot
will show you how the new equipment works and explain some of the principles behind it. North American
has a couple of facilities set up to simulate a SAM site
on their range."

"I don't have my gear."

"No problem," said Pip. "We've got some you can
borrow. It isn't as if this was a combat mission. Just a
demonstration flight."

Osborne shrugged. Lukenbach started across the ramp. Osborne followed Lukenbach into the building. They entered a room off to the right. There were several wall lockers and a couple of benches. Off to one side was a shower room and a latrine. Osborne stood there for a moment and then sat down on the bench. Lukenbach opened one of the lockers.

"Let's get ready."

Osborne nodded and looked up at the colonel. "You sure this is a good idea?"

Lukenbach stared for a moment as if he didn't understand the question. Then he said, "We need something like this. Someone should have been working on it before now."

"Has this really been thought out? I don't want to get involved in something that is going to leave men dead because it was thrown together."

Lukenbach put one foot up on the bench and leaned an elbow on his knee. "Thinking about an antiaircraft-suppression system goes back to the Second World War. We've ignored it until now because the enemy had yet to deploy SAMs and his triple-A was easy to avoid. Now he's got SAMs and we've got to counter them. This flight will show you the value of our system."

"Excuse me, sir, but testing a system against a simulated SAM site is not the same as hitting an enemy target with the bad guys trying to shoot holes in your airplane. That's something the engineers and the brass hats in the Pentagon seem to forget quite often."

"This is the closest to the real thing that we can come up with in this environment. It'll give us a good idea about how the system works."

Osborne nodded and said, "Testing done by the manu-
facturer or the developer of a system is rarely an indication of how the system will function in the field."

"Just go along for the ride. The theories behind the
equipment are sound ones."

"Yes, sir."

Osborne changed into a flight suit and then donned a
G suit. He was given a helmet and a set of new pads for
it. He stripped the paper from the sticky backing and
pressed them into the helmet, adjusting them until the
helmet fit comfortably.

"If you're ready."

They walked back out to the flight line. The test pilot
had already made the preflight and filed the plan with
operations. All that Osborne had to do was climb into
the backseat and let someone else do all the work.

Pip pointed at the test pilot. "This is Tom Ryder, our
chief pilot."

Osborne stuck out his hand. "Paul Osborne."

"Glad to meet you, Major."

"Anything I need to know before we take off?"

"This is a standard F-100. Our modifications are to
the avionics and the wiring throughout, and that's it.
We've got some buffeting, but we've got people working on the problem."

"Okay, then," said Osborne. "I'm ready."

Pip helped Osborne into the rear seat of the plane.
After Osborne climbed into the backseat, Pip climbed
the ladder, standing over Osborne, handing him the various straps for the shoulder harness and seat belt. As
Osborne settled in, Ryder got into the front seat. Ryder
worked through the start-up procedures and, once all

systems were on, Ryder turned and looked into the back.

"You ready?"

"Let's go."

Ryder started to taxi out to the North American runway. He stopped short, cleared with the tower, and then lowered the canopy. The California sun beat down on them, filtering through the canopy and heating the interior. Even the forced air couldn't keep up with the sun.

They taxied onto the runway, and Ryder finished the run-up procedure. He checked his flaps, the settings, and then began the takeoff roll, adding power as they rushed down the runway. About halfway down, they hit transition and rotated, climbing rapidly into the bright blue sky.

Ryder came on the intercom and said, "I'm going to spend a few minutes just flying around up here, letting you get the feel of the airplane."

As he leveled off, the buffeting became noticeable. Ryder was on the intercom again. "We think a minor redesign of the antennae will eliminate the problem."

Osborne said, "Roger." He was looking at the display panels in front of him, and the new control heads.

"We've got a threat panel in the aircraft," said Ryder. "It's the panel that you're not used to seeing. It can discriminate among the various radars to give you an idea of the threat being faced."

"How's that work?" asked Osborne.

"It's based on the different types of radars employed by the enemy. Fan Song signature is different from Long Ear signature. We use that to determine the threat. Signal strength determines distance."

"Okay."

"Now there is a small cathode-ray tube in the center of the panel. It'll give you a direction to the threat. The placement of the antennas, on the fuselage, nose, and tail of the aircraft, allow that."

Osborne studied the cockpit and then nodded. He realized that Ryder wouldn't be able to see that. "Okay."

"If you're ready," said Ryder, "we'll enter the range."

"I'm set."

Ryder rolled over so that the plane was inverted for a moment, then righted himself and dived for the ground. "Watch your threat board and the small screen."

Osborne kept his eyes on the new panel and the screen.

"If there is a SAM launch, the red light will come on." Ryder waited and then said, "We haven't worked out the tactics for attacking the SAM sites or the triple-A threats. We figured to give you the equipment and let you establish the tactics as you need them."

Osborne didn't respond to that. He was trying to get settled in the rear seat and to take in the changes in the cockpit. He studied the board and realized that it would take two men to handle the aircraft. One to fly it and one to watch for the SAMs. The threat board would be too distracting for a single pilot who had to worry about flying the plane at the same time.

"We're about to enter the test area. Flip the switches, they're all marked, and just watch."

They turned suddenly, rolling up on their side so that Osborne, looking to his right, was staring at the ground. The G forces pushed him down into his seat, and then

Ryder rolled out and kicked in the afterburner. Osborne was forced back into his seat.

"Here we go."

The lights on the threat board began to flash, first one and then another, until the red one indicating a SAM launch burned.

"See what I mean?" asked Ryder. "You should have seen lights go on. First from the triple-A and then the SAMs, and finally a launch detection."

"Got them all."

Ryder pulled the nose up and began a rapid climb toward the sun. As he did, he said, sounding just a little winded, "Now the thing to remember is that we're dealing with the radars of the various systems. Doesn't mean that the bad guys are shooting at you, only that they're tracking you. Only when the red light comes on, do you know that they're shooting."

"Unless they're using optically guided guns."

"What?" asked Ryder.

Osborne grinned at the threat panel. "I mean that the North Vietnamese sometimes use 12.7-millimeter weapons that they aim without the benefit of radar. If you're low enough and slow enough, they'll shoot at you with pistols. You won't know that until you see the tracers, or fly into a couple of bullets."

Ryder bent the aircraft around and plunged toward the ground. "Watch your board."

Osborne again saw the lights flash, almost as if a sequence had been programmed into them. He glanced out of the cockpit at the green and brown hillsides around them, but couldn't see the radar sites. They probably weren't much more than transmitters set up to trigger

the threat board. There was no need for the big, spinning receiving antennae because there were no real radar
sites below him. He wondered how the real thing would
look as he raced across the North Vietnamese landscape.

When they completed the second run, Ryder pulled
up again, climbing out. Over the intercom he said, "You
can see how all this works. Any questions?"

"You sure that it's going to be effective over North
Vietnam?"

"The theory is sound," said Ryder. "That's about all I
can tell you."

He turned the aircraft again and flew toward the airfield. There was talk with the control tower and then
ground control, but no other flights were scheduled in.
Ryder ignored downwind legs and crosswind legs and
entered for a straight-in approach. He greased it in so
that there was almost no sensation when the wheels hit
the concrete, and then the drag chute had popped and
they were slowing rapidly.

They turned onto the taxiway, and as they did Osborne saw a jeep sitting there, Lukenbach in the passen-
ger's seat waiting for them. They rolled to a halt and
Ryder opened the canopy, letting in the hot, California
air. As the ladders were leaned against the fuselage, Lukenbach moved out onto the ramp. He stood there,
sweating.

"Well?"

Osborne shrugged. "Theory looks good. Looks very
good, at least on the range."

"Fine. We've a few other things to do, and then you
get on a plane to Eglin."

"Why not just get me a fighter and I'll fly myself. Be there in two, three hours."

"It's not quite that simple."

Osborne pulled off his helmet. "It never is."

Taylor, still wearing his flight suit, the zipper pulled down to his navel, sat across from his commanding officer, Lieutenant Colonel Howard Ott, and waited for the ax to fall. It was a small office with a dirty, plywood floor, plywood walls halfway to the ceiling, and then heavy screens to let in the afternoon breezes. There was a ceiling fan that rotated quickly, blowing air down on them. Ott sat behind a beat-up little gray metal desk and had a dozen plaques on the wall behind him. In the center was a framed award for the Air Medal. That was something of a joke, because pilots in Vietnam were getting so many Air Medals. One Army helicopter pilot, in two tours, had managed to get something like a hundred or more.

Ott leaned back so that his shoulders rested against the plywood of the wall. He locked his fingers behind his head. Short, brown hair covered his head except for bald spots where his helmet pads rested when he flew. It was almost as if the pads had rubbed away the hair, and it gave his head a strange, uneven look.

"Now, why don't you tell me what happened up there?"

Taylor shrugged. "SAM launch from behind us. No one saw it coming and there was nothing that could be done. Even if we had seen it, there would have been no time to evade it. The missile exploded beneath the plane."

"Nothing could be done . . . ?" prompted Ott.

Taylor wiped a hand over his face and said, "Not a damned thing."

"You sure it wasn't an air-to-air missile launched by a fighter from behind you? I've had reports that MiGs were airborne nearby."

"None around us," said Taylor, shaking his head. "Intel has all this."

Ott let the front legs of the chair fall forward, landing with a loud report. He folded his hands together on his desk and stared at Taylor. "I'm just trying to find out why one of my pilots died today. I'll read the intel report, but I want to hear it from you."

Taylor stood up and moved to the side where he could look out on the flight line. There were revetments for the planes, one right after another. Beyond them were the runways where flights of fighters took off for missions in South Vietnam. And there were helicopters, hovering around the edges of the airfield like bees around a field of wild flowers.

"He died because of the restrictions on us. He died because men in Washington decided that SAM sites couldn't be attacked until they launched missiles proving their hostile intent. He died because we have put all the restrictions on ourselves while the enemy is out there without restrictions, waiting for the opportunity to kill us. They're prepared to wage all-out war and we're prepared to let young men die while politicians sit in air-conditioned offices and debate the point."

Ott pointed at the chair opposite him and said, "Sit down and tell me exactly what happened. I need every detail if we're to prevent this from happening again. I'm sorry if this is painful for you, but we need all the information."

Taylor looked at him and thought that the last thing he wanted was to go over it again. He didn't want to relive the sight of the jet exploding. He didn't want to relive the helplessness as they all sat there, in their cockpits, ordering Calhoun out of the jet. All he wanted to do was get out of the office and head for his hootch. Maybe suck down a little bourbon from the bottle there.

But that wasn't what happened. First the intel officer had asked him a hundred questions about the destruction of Calhoun's plane. Now the squadron commander wanted to hear the story. It didn't seem that Taylor was ever going to have the chance to forget about it, if only for a few minutes.

He took a deep breath, rubbed a hand over his sweat-covered face, and dropped into the chair. He closed his eyes as if to gather his thoughts and began to talk, telling Ott about everything that happened from the moment the wheels came off the ground at Tan Son Nhut until they touched down again. Told it all in great detail, mentioning everything that he could remember and even the things that he suspected, so that the commander would understand why one of his pilots had died.

Taylor had not planned to go to the Gunfighter's Club after the debriefing with the commanding officer, but found himself drawn there just the same. The thought of looking at four walls with nothing but a tiny radio and a half-empty bottle of bourbon for company was too much to bear. The mission kept playing itself over and over in his mind, and he began to wonder if there wasn't something that he could have done differently so that no one would have gotten killed.

In the club, he found Dobbs and Hopper sitting at a table, one chair tilted forward with a beer sitting in front of it as a tribute to Calhoun. There was a single chair open, waiting for him. He slipped into it and was handed a beer before he could speak.

"To Calhoun, wherever he might be, whatever he might be doing."

Taylor raised his glass and touched those held by Dobbs and Hopper and said, "To Calhoun."

Taylor took a deep drink and then wiped the beer from his face with the back of his hand. He leaned closer, shouting over the sound of the rock and roll. "Looks like you were wrong, Dobbs."

Dobbs looked at the other man and then nodded. "I was convinced. Absolutely convinced. It just seemed that everything was conspiring against me today. Getting short and getting paranoid, about to die."

Taylor drained his beer and set the glass down. He turned toward the stage just as the dancing girl shed the last of her clothes. He watched her bounce and shake for a moment and then turned back to the men at the table.

Again, as he'd felt in the aircraft flying back to Saigon, he knew there was something to be said. Something about Calhoun, but he was damned if he knew what it was. The man had died and there was nothing that could be done about that now no matter what was said.

He glanced over at the girl as she sank to the floor, rolled to her back, and lifted her legs into the air.

Slowly she spread them so that eveyrone in the club would be able to look directly into her crotch.

He looked away from her and found that neither Dobbs nor Hopper was watching. One naked girl dancing on the stage looked like the next, or the last, and this one was doing nothing that was very interesting.

"There was some good news today," said Taylor.

Both Dobbs and Hopper leaned closer. "What?"

"Boss said that we'd made our last flight to North Vietnam for a while. We stand down for one day and let maintenance get a chance to fix the airplanes, then we're up for close air support missions around here. Nothing too dangerous."

"And then?" asked Dobbs.

Taylor sat quietly for a moment, wishing that they would get the chance to get even with the North Vietnamese. Get a chance to return to North Vietnam with bombs and rockets to attack all the SAM sites and the triple-A defenses.

"And then," he said, shouting over the rock and roll, "maybe we'll get a chance to go back. Not for a while, but I think that's in the cards for the future."

"Good," said Dobbs.

"Yeah," agreed Hopper.

Taylor stood up then. It was not right to watch naked girls dance while Calhoun's body lay rotting in a North Vietnamese rice paddy. Except that the aircraft had disintegrated, so that there was no body to lie rotting.

He shook himself and walked to the door. Ott had promised that the problem of the SAMs was being worked on. It would take a few days, and then something new would be added to the fight. Something that might defeat the SAMs.

"Too late for Calhoun," Taylor had said at the time.

"But that's the way it always is," Ott had then said. "Each development is too late for someone. It's from those deaths that we make our advance."

There was little comfort in that, especially for the families of the men who died, but it wasn't Taylor's fault. As he'd left the colonel's office, he had decided that it was a night to get drunk, but now Taylor didn't feel like making the effort. Maybe it was now just a night to sit quietly and wish that the men in Washington could agree with the men in Hanoi so that men like Calhoun wouldn't have to die.

Taylor realized that he was getting maudlin. Drinking wouldn't help. He headed for his hootch, hoping that he would be able to go to sleep.

# FIVE

**O**SBORNE, after his cross-country flight in the rear of a C-141 Starlifter, was sitting in another briefing room with nine other officers. Four of them were pilots, taken from fighter squadrons around the country, and the other five were electronic warfare officers, pulled mainly from the Strategic Air Command because there weren't many EWOs in the fighter command.

It was much smaller than the briefing room in California, with only a couple of rows of seats, a small stage, and a small screen. There was a podium in one corner of the stage. The walls were cinder block, painted a light green, and there were fluorescent lights overhead, and the buzz of an air conditioner hidden somewhere close by.

Sitting in a separate row behind the pilots and EWOs

were the men who would make up the maintenance ground crews. These were men who had been trained to take care of the F-100 and who had volunteered for a special training session in Florida. With them were a couple of men who were familiar with the new avionics that had been designed in Long Beach.

Lukenbach had been left behind to coordinate with the men at Long Beach who were working to produce more of the Ferret aircraft. Colonel Robert Platte was in charge of the project now that they were at Eglin. Osborne had met the man briefly in base operations, and then had been told where the first briefing would be held. Apparently as each man arrived at Eglin, he received the same orientation.

Platte stepped up to the stage and looked at the men in front of him. He moved to the lectern, glanced at his watch, and the lights faded slightly. The first slide came up and Platte said, "Everything we discuss in this room is classified as secret."

The slides changed and he said, "The first order of business is a change of name. Research has shown that there was a World War Two project called Ferret. We've been redesignated as the Wild Weasels." Platte grinned at the men. "I guess a Wild Weasel is just a nastier form of the ferret."

When there was no immediate reaction to his words, Platte shrugged and said, "This project has only been in the works officially for the last few months. Work was started when the beginnings of SAM-2 sites were identified in North Vietnam. With intelligence briefing us on the capabilities of the SAM, the need for a suppression system was identified."

The slides changed, showing the same things that Osborne had seen in California. Platte felt the need to tell them everything about the SAMs and the development of the system. He moved to the screen, pointed at the slides, told them about the tactics that the SAM operators used against American aircraft. It was a detailed briefing that included a few classified gun-camera pictures of SAMs in flight.

When he finished that, the screen went dark and the lights came on. Platte moved to his podium and leaned on it. "For the purposes of training here at Eglin, we'll be divided into two working groups. Pilots will learn to fly the bird. With all the new equipment and antennae hanging on it, we've got some buffeting problems. Basically, it's still an F-100, it's just that there are a few changes in the overall handling of the aircraft."

One of the maintenance men in the back row stood up. "Sir, Sergeant Donnelly here. I don't think the buffeting has a thing to do with the new antennas. We've had the problem all along with the F-100. The gun barrels vibrate in the tubes, and by using a wooden shim you can dampen it out. Doesn't do a thing to inhibit the accuracy of the weapons and the vibrations are gone."

Platte stood there for a moment, then asked, "Are you sure?"

Donnelly nodded. "Yessir. We've had the trouble all along with them and that always ends it. Been doing that for a couple of years."

"Well, shit," said Platte. "How come that hasn't been sent up the line in the maintenance reports?"

"Could be, sir, that the people up the line don't bother to check with us who are out on the airfield. Guess they figure that if we knew anything, we'd be up there with them, writing all those reports and maintenance advisories and the like."

"Thank you, Sergeant." Platte waited until Donnelly sat down and then shook his head. "What a fucking way to run things."

He consulted his notes and said, "Pilots and EWOs will get a quick orientation here, and then we'll go out to the flight line so that you all can see the aircraft and the modifications to them. Ground crews will be taken out to the hangar area so that you can get a look at the new avionics packages and the configuration of the antennas. Questions?"

No one spoke, so Platte divided the men into their training groups. Platte then began a quick briefing on the aircraft. Platte also told them they had been brought to Eglin because Eglin had a range equipped with a Soviet air defense simulator known locally as a SADS. The simulator could be turned to a variety of frequencies to simulate different Soviet weapons systems. The flight crews would be flying a morning mission package and then an afternoon package. Each package would simulate the actual missions as they would probably be flown in Vietnam.

Using slides that showed the range, Platte, using a light arrow, talked them through a sample mission. "You will fly toward the SADS until the threat board lights up. The backseat will talk to the pilot until the site is acquired visually, and then you will simulate an attack run on the site. To practice, ingress and egress will be from different directions."

Platte set the light arrow down and turned up the

lights. As the last slide faded, he said, "Ground crews will be studying the new equipment while the air crews are flying. Ground crews will be responsible for the aircraft assigned to this project. Questions?"

"When's this all begin?" asked Osborne.

"Theories and classwork right after lunch and first mission package tomorrow with a takeoff time of 0830 hours. Anything else?"

Platte waited, looking into the faces of each of the men, who sat there quietly. Finally he said, "I want the ground crews to move to room 406. Flight crews remain here and get to know one another." Platte left the stage then and exited to the hallway as the enlisted men and the maintenance officer stood up to leave.

When everyone was gone, Osborne sat there for a moment, looking at the captains and lieutenants thrown in with him. He stood up and surveyed the men, the boys really. Young men who had been out of college no more than two or three years and who had found themselves sucked up into the great war machine. It was one of the ironies of life.

He moved to the front and said, "I'm Major Osborne and I haven't the faintest idea of what the hell they expect us to do, but as the senior officer here, I guess I'm supposed to say something."

"Sir," said one of the lieutenants, "I'm Richard Hertz and I"—he glanced at the other men—"most of us, don't have any idea what the hell is going on."

"Didn't you listen to the briefing?"

"Yessir. What did it mean?"

Osborne rubbed his chin and grinned at the men. "I

understand that most of you are volunteers—given the chance to volunteer for special training?"

"Yessir," said Hertz.

"Didn't any of you know what the hell you were volunteering for?"

"No, sir. Other than, as you said, special training in Florida."

Osborne looked at the men again and shook his head. "Gentlemen, I think that each and everyone of you has just volunteered for a tour in Vietnam, just as soon as the training here has been completed."

"Oh, shit," said Hertz.

"Exactly," said Osborne.

The afternoon session didn't tell them much more. They sat at small, two-man tables, while Platte and then a maintenance officer who didn't bother to introduce himself lectured them on the F-100 and the new equipment. Although the briefing was designed for the EWOs, the pilots were forced to sit through it too, so that they would be familiar with the new instrumentation in the aircraft.

When they finished, Platte took the stage and said, "Tomorrow, briefings begin at 0600. Tonight you're on your own, but remember tomorrow there will be flights scheduled."

He stood there for a moment, looking into the faces of the men. It seemed that there was something more that he wanted to say to them, but he didn't. Finally he shrugged, as if in defeat, and left. As he disappeared out the door, Osborne, still the unofficial commander of the unit, asked, "Who the hell has a car around here?"

Hertz and another lieutenant, Thomas Kenyon, raised their hands. Kenyon added, "I was stationed here already, so I've got my POV."

"Okay," said Osborne. "Florida is known for its seafood. I suggest that we take an hour to get changed into civilian clothes, and meet for dinner. Kenyon, you and Hertz get to drive since you were clever enough to get here with cars. Anyone object to the plan?"

There was silence for a moment and Osborne added, "Gentlemen, if I've got this figured right, we're going to be forming the core of a new unit and it'll be best if we get to know each other here, in Florida, rather than in Vietnam with people shooting at us. Since we probably don't have much time to do that, we'd better start now."

"An hour," said Hertz.

"Right. Anyone object?"

When no one spoke, Osborne said, "Then one hour."

They assembled in the parking lot outside the VOQ, the men introducing themselves to one another quickly. Osborne tried to catch the names, but could only remember Kenyon and Hertz.

With that done, they managed to cram the ten men into the two cars. Osborne told Kenyon to find them a good restaurant with a selection of seafood. They drove out the gate, down a highway that was lined with tall trees, and through a town. They crossed a raised bridge over a wide river that led out to the Gulf of Mexico, and then entered another small town. They worked their way around, using the back streets until they came to a long, low building that was painted white and had a green awning on the front of it. There was a huge parking lot, graveled and bordered by short, green bushes.

As they got out of the cars, Kenyon waved at the place. "Best food around here."

Osborne stared at the parking lot, which was almost empty. Two cars and a pickup truck.

Kenyon caught the glance and said, "It's a little early for the dinner crowd. Place will begin to fill up about seven-thirty and then you won't be able to get a table until nine, ten o'clock. I've had to wait three hours to get seated when I haven't timed it right."

Osborne nodded. That was the thing about the military. Everything on a schedule and that schedule was an hour or two earlier than those of the civilian world. That was why the day at military bases started at seven and ended at four and sometimes earlier than that. Lunch was at eleven or eleven-thirty. Out of sync with the civilians.

They entered. There was a small foyer with a glass case and a cash register. A woman sat behind it, ignoring everything as she read a magazine. The hostess, a young woman with long blond hair, appeared and directed them to the rear, where there were several big tables already set for large groups. For no good reason, Osborne had expected a view of the water. Instead they had a view of the rear parking lot, slightly smaller than the one in the front.

The interior was decorated with fishnets, glass floats, and mounted fish. There were pictures of sailing ships, and there were glass tanks holding fish, some to be eaten and some to be watched.

The men sat down, and a moment later a waitress

handed each of them a menu. As she finished passing them out, she asked, "Would anyone care for anything from the bar before you order dinner?"

Osborne laughed, and Kenyon said, "Of course we'd like something from the bar."

She went around the table, writing down the drink orders—everything from an old-fashioned to a bottle of beer. While she was gone, the men studied the menus. Then she was back handing out the drinks and trying to ignore the comments made by the men. When she was done and had left, Osborne got to his feet. "I haven't had the chance to talk to each of you yet, but that will come. Now, I'd just like to say that we've got the opportunity to develop a concept from the ground up. That's an opportunity that few men in our positions ever have. Everything we do will be new and innovative. Just as it should be."

One by one the men got to their feet, and they all drank. Then, as they sat down, Kenyon said, "To the Air Force." They all drank again.

After dinner, they went around the table introducing themselves again, Osborne leading off and talking a little about his background. Thomas Kenyon was next, followed by David Froiseth, Jack H. Daniels, who made sure that each of them understood he always used his middle initial, then Richard Hertz, Tim Casey, Edward Benning, Tom Waters, Larry Boyle, and then finishing with Lieutenant Jerry Dallas, who was the youngest man there. Each told a story that was similar. A love of flying that led them into the Air Force, where the government would pay them to fly airplanes.

With the introductions finished, Osborne asked Kenyon to recommend a local night spot. Kenyon led them to a dark club that was filled with tables, and had a small lighted stage and women who took off their clothes in time to the rock-and-roll music. It was hot and smoky inside, but it was what the men wanted.

Osborne would have preferred to have gone somewhere else for the after-dinner drinks. Watching college-age girls strip wasn't something he enjoyed all that much, but the younger men had organized the trip. Watching the girls only made him feel his age. It had seemed that it was only yesterday that he had been in college, chasing women, and now they all looked young enough to be his daughters. Not that he was that much older than the others, he just felt that way.

But Osborne had felt that he should accompany them to build a spirit of camaraderie, although he couldn't have explained why he felt that way. Let them know that he was one of the boys, even if he didn't feel like it.

He sat there, at the end of the table, nursing a drink as the show got wilder and the girls danced in the nude. No longer were they wearing G-strings or pasties. Those had been left behind. One of them used a towel as a prop, rubbing it between her legs and then waving it at the audience. She was trying to get a response from the men with Osborne.

As she finished one set, she walked over and crouched, letting each of the men examine her closely, turning and twisting in front of them. She smiled at each in turn and said, "What do you fellows do for a living?"

Kenyon grinned right back and said, "We're cops."

The expression on the dancer's face held for just an

instant and then broke. She glanced over her shoulder as if looking for support and then put up one arm as if trying to cover her naked breasts. Sweat blossomed and dripped down the sides of her face, between her breasts, across her belly.

The music died as the girl stood up, unsure of what to do. She looked to the rear and in a stage whisper said, "They're cops."

Everyone in the club heard what she said. Two men leaped up and headed for the door. A second later, another man stumbled as he tried to get out of his chair so that he could leave. In less than a minute, nearly everyone had fled through the door, and only Osborne and the men with him were left.

"Shit," said Kenyon, "I was only kidding." But she didn't hear him.

She disappeared through the curtain at the rear of the stage. A moment later the music came back on, but the lights over the stage went out.

"Nice job," said Osborne.

"Laws in the state of Florida," said Kenyon, "prohibit complete nudity."

"So?" asked Hertz.

Kenyon looked at him and said, "It was just a little joke. That's all."

A man peered through the curtain, seemed to search the room as if looking for someone, and then came out on the stage. He walked over to where Osborne and the others sat and said, "We certainly appreciate your business . . . but next time, could you not announce it?"

Osborne smiled at the man and asked, "Why not? We're just here for a little beer and a little music."

The manager nodded and continued to smile. He stood up and pointed at the bartender. "Bring these gentlemen anything they would like to drink. This round is on us."

"Thank you," said Osborne.

The manager left and the next girl came out to dance. Slowly she removed her top layer of clothes, revealing a tiny bra and bikini panties, but she refused to take them off. The tone of the show changed, too. There was no longer an undercurrent of sexuality in it. Just pretty girls in bikinis dancing to hard-driving rock and roll.

Kenyon looked at his watch as the second girl finished not taking off her clothes. "Getting pretty late."

Osborne leaned close to him and said, "I feel guilty about clearing out the place. Least we can do is stay until the end of the shows and buy some drinks."

"But we have to fly tomorrow," said Kenyon.

Osborne looked at his watch and said, "Regulations say that we can't drink eight hours before a flight. Given the normal procedures and preflights, we shouldn't be airborne before nine. That gives us twenty minutes to drink."

The waitress came back, got their orders, and then went away. When she returned, Osborne gave her a ten-dollar tip and said, "Thanks."

The classroom work in the morning took only thirty minutes. Osborne sat there, a cup of coffee in front of him and a doughnut on a paper towel by his hand. He was studying a map that had the attack routes marked on it.

Kenyon dropped into the chair next to him and said, "I have a big head this morning. Fucking huge."

"Beer will do that," said Osborne. He glanced at the younger man. Sandy hair, blue eyes that seemed to be dull today, a deep tan, and almost no trace of a beard.

"I quit drinking beer and switched to bourbon."

"Christ, man," said Osborne, "that's a combination that can kill. You've got to be careful."

Kenyon looked at Osborne's coffee cup and then at the pot sitting on a small table not far away. He got up, pulled a Styrofoam cup off the stack, and filled it. He took one drink, made a face, and took another, longer one. He then refilled the cup, added sugar and cream, and sat down next to Osborne.

"What you got?"

"Flight route through the range. We're scheduled for takeoff in about two and a half hours."

"Good. If I'm not dead by then, I should be able to fly," said Kenyon.

Osborne looked up from his map and noticed that the other men had already paired off. He hadn't said a word to any of them and was sure that Platte had not designed the roster. It was strange, they had all known one another for just over twenty-four hours, and already they had figured out the crews for themselves. Not one word had been said.

On a mission like this, with the man in the backseat having to depend on the skills of the pilots, and with the pilots depending on the EWOs, you needed men who trusted each other. If they were friends, that would be better. They had to work together flawlessly, like some kind of well-oiled machine. If the men had preferences,

Osborne would let those preferences stand unless they conflicted with the mission.

That was, of course, if he was tapped as the commander. Since there was no one in the room who outranked him, he figured that he would get the nod. That explained the orientation flight in Long Beach. Someone at the top had thought his way through the whole problem—or at least the command structure of it—before he had shoved people into the slots.

"You understand everything about the threat panel and the electronic readings?" asked Osborne.

"Nothing to understand, really," said Kenyon. He drank from his cup and added. "It's all labeled. The only area open to interpretation is the cathode-ray tube, and that's fairly straightforward."

Osborne showed him the flight route, and gave him a briefing on the terrain. Kenyon grinned and said, "I live here, Major. I'm familiar with the ranges already."

"Good. We shouldn't have any trouble then."

When they had finished their coffee and Osborne his doughnut, they picked up their flight gear and headed down to the aircraft. Unlike most fighters at Eglin, the F-100s modified for the Wild Weasel mission were sitting inside the hangar. The aircraft wouldn't be wheeled out until it was time to take off for the range.

Osborne walked around the aircraft, looking at it. Then he began a serious preflight while the crew chief stood close by and watched. Osborne opened access panels, and checked hatches and doors, mountings and avionics. With Kenyon at his side, he poked his nose everywhere, looking for a mistake made by someone else that could kill him if he missed it.

When he finished, the hangar doors were opened. There was a loud buzz from a Klaxon, and the doors rumbled along their rail, slowly letting in the Florida humidity and sunshine. A yellow tug, driven by an Air Force master sergeant in fatigues, rolled in. The crew chief hooked the nose wheel of the F-100 to the tug and the plane was towed out into the morning sun.

"If you're ready," said Osborne.

"Any time," said Kenyon.

Osborne watched as two other crews went through the same ritual. Just as they were about to leave, Platte arrived. He whistled once and waved everyone over to him.

"One thing you should know, when you hit the range, all other activity will cease. We don't want anyone else seeing your planes and speculating about your mission. This whole thing is very hush-hush."

Osborne rubbed a hand through his hair. "Won't pulling everyone else from the range cause the speculation you're trying so hard to avoid?"

"Doesn't matter, if they haven't seen the planes. Besides, the people around here are used to having experimental aircraft out there. It won't be a problem. When you get back, we'll debrief in the classroom."

Kenyon started to raise a hand and then announced, "I'm going to the can now. Always have to go a final time before takeoff."

"Hurry it up," said Platte.

Kenyon trotted off across the hangar floor. Osborne waited for Platte to speak again, but the man had fallen silent. Platte stepped back to the edge of the hangar, inside the yellow lines that marked the walkways near the wall.

Osborne watched the other crews head out to their aircraft. For a moment he hesitated, and then followed them, figuring that Kenyon could catch up later. As he climbed into the cockpit, he saw Kenyon coming toward him at a slow jog.

Kenyon climbed into the rear seat and began strapping himself in as the crew chief removed the ladders. As Kenyon finished, Osborne cranked the engine, while the crew chief stood close to a large fire extinguisher in case of fire.

Osborne wound up the engine and then began to taxi, moving from the ramp in front of the hangar, then along the ramp's edge, passing parked aircraft and reaching the taxiway. He held there, contacted ground control, and was cleared to taxi to the active runway.

Osborne then contacted the tower and was cleared for the runway. He lowered the canopy and taxied into position. A moment later they were roaring along the ground, gaining speed, the force pushing them back into their seats. Osborne hauled back on the stick and they climbed skyward.

The mission package was almost a repeat of the one Osborne had flown in California. Kenyon kept his head buried in the back, looking for indications that they were being tracked by the SADS radars. They rolled through the range at altitude as Kenyon searched the ground for the enemy. When Kenyon picked up the radar signals, he called them out, telling Osborne the direction to fly. Together they searched the ground, looking for the simulated enemy radar site.

They finished the morning mission package without making a single gun run. The plan was to familiarize the guy in the backseat with the new equipment and let the pilot know how the aircraft handled with the modifications to the airframe. It was almost the same as boring holes in the sky for the purpose of getting flight time. The morning mission wasn't quite that bad, and it did have a destination and an objective. It wasn't as bad as being told to get three hours of flight time. Here they just had to complete the mission and head back to their airfield for landing.

Osborne finally cleared the range and climbed up to fifteen thousand feet. He hung there for a few minutes, looking to the south where the Gulf of Mexico was spread out all the way to the horizon, like a blue-green stained glass window lying on the ground in the distance. He thought about the South China Sea and where they would all be in a month or less. He forced the thought from his mind.

Finally, over the intercom, he said, "You ready to return to the barn?"

Kenyon looked at his threat board. Two of the lights and the CRT showed that SAM sites were operating, but both were out of range of the F-100's weapons. Kenyon wasn't sure about the range of the SA-2. In Vietnam, that was a piece of information he'd make sure he had.

"I'm ready," he said.

Osborne turned the aircraft over and dived for the ground. He rolled out and made the first of the radio calls to the tower. It wouldn't be long before they were on the ground and sucking down a cold one.

# SIX

ON the day of the maintenance stand-down, Taylor didn't feel like working. Every aviation unit, every military unit moved on paperwork, regardless of what Napoléon might have said. The paperwork came in great blizzards of triplicate forms that threatened to bury everything under their relentless progress. Everyone in the military always had paperwork to fill out, from the highest general to the lowest private. When the paperwork had nothing to do with the administration of the unit, there was paperwork that related to the individual and his position in the unit and in the Air Force.

A ton of it, maybe more, waited for Taylor, but he had no desire to do any of it. If it didn't get done, there would be a letter from a higher headquarters telling him that some periodic report hadn't been completed, and he would already know that because he was the one who hadn't filled out the report. Instead of sitting at the wobbly field desk painted a hideous green as if that would camouflage it in the jungle, and fighting his way through the paper, he opted to sit in the air-conditioned Gunfighter's Club and fight his way through a glass of beer.

At first there was only Taylor, sitting near the stage, the bartender who had come in early to count the receipts and finish his paperwork, and one waitress whose turn it was to clean up. She was wiping down the tables with a wet rag when Taylor entered.

Taylor ordered a single beer, got a glass of it, and then sat down. He stared at the stage as if he expected a woman to appear there at any moment. Then he sipped his beer slowly and ignored everything around him, including the waitress, who wasn't working very hard.

About the time he finished his first beer, the waitress sat down at the table and then moved around so that Taylor could see her legs. As she had sat down, she had managed to hike her skirt even higher, leaving very little to the imagination.

"You buy me beer?" she asked.

Taylor looked at her and wondered if it was some kind of racket like those run in the bars on Tu Do Street. The girls drank Saigon Tea at two or three dollars a glass, calling it champagne. It was actually a weak tea. The Gunfighter's Club was supposed to be above that sort of thing. It didn't have a civilian owner who wanted to make as much money as he could as quickly as he could.

"I'll buy you a beer if I can get another one."

She smiled at him, showing pearly white teeth that surprised him. Most Vietnamese had pointed teeth from eating sugar cane or blackened teeth from eating betel nuts. She jumped up and ran to the bar, then returned, setting the two sweat-beaded cans on the table.

"You here early."

"Yes, well, we have a day down." He regretted saying that, because it was a bit of intelligence that she didn't need. But then, he didn't know who she could tell and what good it could do them.

She pulled her chair closer and leaned toward him. He could see a light coating of perspiration on her skin. Beads of it on her upper lip and at her hairline.

"What your name, Joe?"

Taylor looked at her for a moment, wishing that she would go away. She was like a stewardess on a flight. Wasn't happy unless she was serving everyone in some fashion. Handing out beverages, feeding passengers, giving them pillows and blankets and magazines. Now, like a stewardess, the waitress wouldn't leave him alone. She wanted to serve.

"Bill. You can call me Bill."

"I like that name, Bill."

"What's your name?" Taylor asked.

"Linda."

Taylor stared at her. She was obviously Vietnamese, and if there was any French blood in her veins, it had been diluted by several generations. That meant she had chosen the name herself to please the GIs.

"Well, Linda, what's new?"

"I don't understand. New?"

Taylor sat there for a moment, trying to think of a

way to explain the question to her, and couldn't figure it out. Her English was fairly good, but she didn't understand the slang. Taylor sipped his beer and waited.

"What you do, Bill?"

Taylor debated saying, because he'd sat in enough briefings telling him that everyone in Vietnam, with the exception of other Americans, was not to be trusted. In fact, the number of trustworthy individuals had been cut even more when he had been told not to trust reporters, people at the embassy, and civilian contractors. The intel officer, ever security-conscious, had said that the smallest piece of information, coupled with other small, seemingly insignificant bits, could add up to a complete picture, giving the enemy the advantage. But then, Taylor was in the Gunfighter's Club, which gave her a clue about his job anyway. And when he wore his uniform in, that provided clues too, if she was inclined to search for clues. In other words, he decided that it didn't matter what he told her.

"I fly airplanes."

"Big ones or little ones?"

"Some of both," he said. He glanced at the bartender, who was busy counting bottles. He had hoped the man would save him, but knew that he wouldn't. He would assume that Taylor liked the company.

"I'm off now," said Linda. "I go home. You want to come with me?"

Taylor looked at her closely. A slender, almost tiny girl, she had jet-black hair, dark brown eyes, and a nearly perfect complexion. He sat there, staring, thinking quickly. He thought about Calhoun's jet exploding over North Vietnam and how death lurked so close that it was almost like an old friend. He thought about the fear that stood next to death, and thought about keeping his mind occupied with activities. Anything to fill it up and keep him busy. He was caught off guard by the question, but then, he was supposed to be quick on his feet. All pilots were supposed to be quick.

He drained his beer and set the glass on the table, deciding that drinking alone was not the answer to his depression. "Sure, I'd like to go with you."

She stood up and said, "You wait here. I come back real fast."

"Okay."

She bent over to kiss him, and as she did he was able to look down her blouse. She wasn't wearing a bra, but with her small breasts, she didn't need one. He caught her looking at him looking at her, and he knew what she was doing. Giving him a view to keep him interested. She smiled broadly.

"I hurry."

As he watched her retreat, he tried to figure out what had happened. He hadn't been interested in a date and now he had one. He'd somehow lost control of the situation, but wasn't at all sure that he cared. Sometimes it was necessary to let things get away. He'd wait to see how things developed.

They left the Gunfighter's Club and walked along the paved streets of Tan Son Nhut, near the area known as Hotel Three. They didn't enter the gate that would have taken them to the BX run by the Air Force or given them access to Hotel Three. Instead they turned the other direction and walked to the main gate so that they could leave the base. Outside the base, on the street,

Taylor only had to raise a hand and a taxi dived out of the traffic, sliding toward him. As it neared the curve, the taxi's rear door popped open. The Vietnamese driver wasn't watching the street. He was leaning over the back of the seat to open the door.

Linda got in first and then Taylor followed. Once he was inside, the woman moved closer to him and then took his elbow in both her hands. The driver grinned at them and asked something in Vietnamese. When Linda answered him, he nodded and grinned broadly, his mouth full of broken, yellowed teeth. He then laughed at her.

"What'd he say?"

"He want to know where we go. I told him and he take us there now."

"And where are we going?" asked Taylor, suddenly sure that he was the victim of some elaborate VC trap.

"We go to my house."

Taylor nodded and then turned to look out. They were on a wide, palm-lined street that was filled with cars, trucks, jeeps, Lambrettas, and motorbikes. There were a few pedicabs and quite a few pedestrians. There were military men and civilians. Women, some dressed in the traditional *ao dai*, and more dressed in short skirts and tight blouses. The air was hot, and heavy with moisture. The fumes from the engines seemed to hang in the street, as if it were a poison gas that had been sprayed out to kill the pedestrians. The air somehow looked brown and dirty.

And there was noise. The sound of engines, the roar of jets overhead, along with the pop of rotorblades from helicopters. People were shouting at one another, and there was music from radios and from bars.

They left the wide, beautiful street and turned down another that wasn't wide, palm-lined, or neat. There were potholes in it, and no shoulders. The buildings, which had looked to be of French design, gave way to older houses—small things with tile roofs and small yards. There was a new odor added to all the others. One of unwashed bodies and sewers.

The car stopped and the driver turned, still grinning. He held out a hand and said, "You give me one thousand P. You give me now."

Taylor knew that the price was inflated but didn't feel like haggling over it. The man wanted just under ten dollars for the ride. Extreme but not unheard of. Besides, to him, it was little more than pennies.

Linda said something in Vietnamese, a quick, short sentence in the singsong language. The smile on the man's face faded slightly.

"You give me five hundred P."

Taylor dug in his wallet and found some of the Vietnamese money. He paid the driver. Linda opened the door and slipped out and then reached back to drag Taylor with her. As he got out, the car roared off, leaving them alone.

Taylor realized that he was in the middle of a Vietnamese neighborhood, alone and unarmed. No one at the base knew where he was, though the bartender, if pressed, might be able to figure it out.

He stood there for a moment and looked at the dilapidated hootch in front of him. If he had been in the southwestern United States, he would have believed that it was adobe—it was built of a dung-colored stone, and had windows on either side of a door. One of the windows was covered by a sheet of plywood. A broken sidewalk led to the front door. No grass had been planted, though there were a couple of bushes at the side of the house. They had thick, green leaves and tiny, multicolored blossoms.

"You come on," said Linda, taking his hand.

Taylor allowed himself to be led inside. It was hot and musty in the house. Linda disappeared and there was a quiet roar as a fan began to blow, circulating the hot air. Linda returned and asked, "You want drink?"

"Okay," said Taylor.

"You sit down."

Taylor moved from the door to one of the rooms, surprised by the western furniture in it. He'd expected bamboo mats and low tables, maybe something like the interiors of houses in Japan. Instead there were chairs, a long, low sofa, and a couple of tables. On one was a record player from the BX and a number of albums containing the music of American rock-and-roll singers.

Linda returned and handed him a glass containing a dark liquid and a few chunks of ice. Not the cubes that he was used to seeing, but miniature icebergs that looked chipped from a larger block of ice. He tasted the beverage and was surprised to find that it was Coke.

Linda sat down opposite him and slowly crossed her legs, letting her skirt ride high on her thighs, displaying them. "You like?"

Taylor gulped at his drink as he wondered why he had allowed this to happen. He said, "Yes. Very much."

"It hot." Linda smiled and set her glass on the table.

She reached up and unbuttoned the top of her blouse, using both hands. She did it slowly, as if unsure how the buttons worked. When she finished, she pulled the blouse open just far enough to show the swell of her tiny breasts and the smoothness of her chest and stomach. A bead of perspiration dripped, rolling slowly between her breasts, heading for her belly button. She stopped it with her index finger and then licked the finger clean, her tongue curling around it as she did so. She kept her eyes on Taylor.

Taylor had watched a number of women try to act sexy. He'd seen them try to strip slowly and erotically, watched them dance naked, and watched them as they tried to turn him on using their hands on their bodies. They'd tried a lot of different things, and he could never remember anyone succeeding quite as quickly as Linda. That one act, licking the sweat from her own finger, had done it all. He didn't know what it was, but he felt his desire grow rock hard, and he wished that he hadn't come to her house.

Now Linda leaned forward to pick up her glass. Her blouse fell open, showing her breasts. Small but perfectly shaped, they had button-sized areolae and hard, pointed nipples. She looked to be as excited as he was.

Taylor started to stand up and then realized that he couldn't. Not without embarrassing himself. He crossed his legs and grinned sheepishly.

Linda took a drink and again set down her glass. She stood and reached for the zipper of her skirt. She eased it down but held the garment in place. She hesitated for a moment, then let go. The skirt slipped over her hips and pooled on the floor at her feet.

She wore skimpy panties made of white lace. They concealed almost nothing. She shrugged her shoulders and the blouse joined the skirt.

"You like?" she asked again.

Taylor examined her body the way he would an aircraft before flying it. He started at her feet, partially concealed by the discarded clothes. Her ankles were trim, almost delicate. Her calves were slightly muscled, as were her thighs. Delicate lines and delicate curves shaped her legs. There was a flare at the hips and then a tiny waist. Her stomach was flat. Her breasts were proportioned to her body.

"Very much," repeated Taylor.

She hooked her thumbs in the waistband of the panties and rolled them down her thighs to her knees. She straightened up, leaving the panties at her knees. She grinned at him, scissored her legs and her panties slid down around her ankles. She stepped out of them, leaving them on top of the pile of her clothing.

"I like you," she said. "We go upstairs now."

Taylor wasn't sure about that. She stared at him, and he was sure that she wanted something more from him. Information about his unit to sell to the enemy. Something about the pilots who flew the missions or the capabilities of the aircraft they had. Something.

Instead, she came to him and knelt beside him. She took the glass from his hand and put it on the floor. She unbuttoned his shirt and then leaned over him, kissing his bare chest, using her tongue to trace shapes on his skin. she glanced up, smiled, and went back to work. She unbuckled his belt and worked at the zipper of his fly.

Taylor was on the verge of telling her to stop. He wanted her to stop long enough for him to think. He'd let events take their own course without a thought about it, never reacting to the situations thrown at him. That was in contrast to his normal attitude, where he controlled everything all the time.

Now she slid a hand down and grabbed him. Her fingers were cool, and he knew it was too late to stop her. There was no way that he would be able to stop her.

Finally Taylor stood up, and she slipped his clothes from him rapidly, so that he stood naked in front of her. She was still on her knees, kissing him, her lips cool on his body. If it was a trick, he thought, then it was time for the trap to spring shut, but that didn't happen. No one came rushing at him with a weapon, demanding to know what was going on.

"We go upstairs now?"

Taylor looked at the pile of clothes. It contained his wallet, with his ID card, credit cards, cards for a number of professional organizations—a real treasure trove for an enemy agent. He wasn't sure if she was trying to separate him from his clothes for that reason or not, but decided not to take the chance. He picked her up, surprised at how light she was, and carried her to the sofa. Gently he set her down and waited as she settled.

"You nice," she said.

Taylor wasn't sure if he was nice or not, but wasn't about to get into an argument about it. He knelt on the sofa between her knees and then stretched out, kissing her on the lips for the first time.

\* \* \*

An hour later, Taylor felt much better. He was as bathed in sweat as was Linda. They lay together, side by side, arm in arm, on her sofa. She was asleep, her breathing slow and rhythmic now that they had finished.

Taylor was able to see his watch and the sweep second hand as it moved around and around. He felt the passing of time, saw it, and didn't care. Tomorrow would be soon enough to get back into things, back into the war. Get to the paperwork that the clerks and bureaucrats couldn't live without.

As he watched the Vietnamese girl sleep, he realized something that civilians didn't. There were no weekends in war. Just endless Mondays that seemed to blend together into one long, drawn-out workday. There wasn't any time off for good behavior—in fact, the only time off he ever had was that which he stole. Instead of sitting at his desk, doing his paperwork as he should, where they could find him, he had slipped away to enjoy himself for a couple of hours. It was the only time of relaxation that he got. The stolen moments.

He grinned and almost laughed. It was funny how such a simple act could take the edge off so easily and completely. He had been depressed, drinking, and ready to punch out the first person, man or woman, who looked at him cross-eyed. His stomach had been churning and he hadn't been eating right. Suddenly he was hungry, relaxed, almost happy.

Linda stirred and opened one eye. She studied Taylor's face for a moment and then said, "You look better, Bill."

"I feel better."

"I go back to work now." She moved slightly, her

hips against him. There was a slight pressure against his crotch as she moved.

Taylor felt himself respond quickly and almost painfully. It was as if he were an eighteen-year-old kid again who had never done it before and suddenly couldn't get enough of it. He let one hand slide along her naked flank, feeling the textures and softness of her skin. There was a catch in her breathing as he touched her.

Linda felt him grow and smiled. She lifted one leg up and reached down with her hand to grasp him. She was more than ready for him as he pushed against her.

"I go to work later," she said quietly. "I do not have to go right now."

"Glad to hear it."

# SEVEN

DOBBS led the flight of four. Hopper was his wingman and Edward Doyle was the element leader, with Paul Augustine flying in the slot. It was a scraped-together flight from the beginning, since it had been a mission laid on late after the stand-down order had been issued. The frag had come down late, and by the time the unit's mission had been broken out, many of the pilots had scattered into Saigon for a day on the town. Those who hadn't learned quickly that they should have gotten out before the brass found something for them to do were now stuck.

Dobbs hadn't liked being elevated to the roll of flight leader. It was easy to sit back, as a wingman, and let the other guy worry about the navigation, the weather conditions at takeoff, the tanker's location, the weather over the target, and all the other problems. It was much easier to sit there and complain than it was to find yourself leading the flight.

But then, Dobbs had found the tanker—a simple task as the men in the tanker had vectored them in until they spotted the big KC-135 orbiting far out over the South China Sea.

And the weather hadn't been a problem. Winds at takeoff had been almost nonexistent, and there were only high, thin, scattered clouds. It was a warm day, with a high-density altitude, which meant that it took a longer runway roll to get the heavy fighters off the ground, but that was why the runways at Tan Son Nhut had been lengthened years before.

The Doppler navigation system, when it worked, made that task easier, and the second element leader was supposed to be paying attention in case it didn't. Dobbs was pleased because the only mistake he'd made so far was one that no one but him knew about. A minor thing and he'd never mention it, so it was as if it hadn't happened.

With the tanker rendezvous out of the way, they began their flight into North Vietnam, and suddenly Dobbs was no longer quite as confident. The enemy would be out there waiting, with the express purpose of shooting holes in his aircraft and his body. And the weather was good enough that they'd have to worry about MiGs, too. The enemy would be all over the place.

As they crossed the coastline, from the relative safety of the South China Sea to the relative danger of North Vietnam, Dobbs keyed his mike and said, "Wasp, check."

"Two."

"Three."

"Four."

Around him, in the skies over North Vietnam, he heard other flights running through the same routine. Everyone making sure that his whole flight had made it to their target. In ten or twenty minutes, when the shooting started, the air would be full of checks as well as enemy bullets and missiles.

"Let's clean them up," said Dobbs. Suddenly he felt scared. He was in command. Before, when the order had been passed, he'd felt a twinge in his stomach, but now it seemed that someone had tied it in a knot. No longer was the mission someone else's responsibility. Now it was his. His mistakes could kill, his decisions could kill. There was no one there to tell him what to do or what not to do. It was all up to him.

"Wasps, we have weak guns," said someone. Dobbs thought that it was Doyle.

"Roger guns."

Off to the right, at ten o'clock, there were scattered puffs of black smoke. It was a klick off, poorly aimed, and maybe not even directed at him.

They continued on, listening as the other flights attacked their targets. There were calls about SAMs and enemy guns. Dobbs kept his eyes open but didn't see anything directed at them.

"SAMs coming up!"

Dobbs didn't recognize the voice.

"Whose got the SAMs?"

"Saturn, take it down."

"Detroit, breaking right."

"Saturn's got SAMs at two o'clock. Let's lose the tanks."

"Detroit, light your burners."

"Saturn, Saturn, we have two MiG-21s at ten o'clock."

"Saturn, go to afterburners, now."

Mission requirements and mission secrecy meant that Dobbs didn't know where the two flights who were having trouble were located. They were somewhere not too far away, out of sight, but the radio signals were strong.

"Stinger, you have one behind you. Break now! Go to burners."

Dobbs wanted to get into the fight, but didn't know exactly where it was. He kept to the preprogrammed heading, watching the sky, watching the ground, trying to keep his eyes on everything around him.

"Guns to the front."

Dobbs saw a string of tracers rocket past him—great glowing red balls streaking upward. He tried to look down at the ground to spot the weapon, but passed it too fast, the tracers suddenly behind him.

"Stinger, I got him! I got him!"

"Good shot. Look at the son of a bitch burn."

"There's one on your tail."

Dobbs twisted around, looking until he realized that it wasn't him. Someone had made a blind call and now every American pilot over North Vietnam would be looking for the enemy fighter that wasn't there.

"Stinger, he's on your tail."

Dobbs relaxed then, but it wasn't for long.

"Wasp, we have guns at one o'clock and three o'clock, all firing."

Dobbs saw the first puffs from the flak, off to his right, almost too far away to see. But they started coming closer and closer. Dobbs began a slow descent, just to throw them off, bleeding off his altitude and then beginning a slow climb.

"SAMs!"

There was nothing around Dobbs. He kept his eyes moving, from his instruments to the Doppler, and outside the cockpit. In the distance he spotted two aircraft coming at him. Since they were pointed at him, he assumed they were hostile. They were too far off to identify.

"Coming up at eleven o'clock," said someone.

"Got 'em," said Dobbs.

Then the flak was bursting all around them. They were buffeted by it, bouncing around. Shrapnel rattled against the aircraft. The jets that had been coming at them turned, racing away. As they rocked up on their sides for the turn, Dobbs caught a glimpse of the pointed nose and the delta wings. MiG-21s, though the Phantom sometimes looked like the 21 if the angle and the light were right.

"MiGs on the run."

"SAM! SAM! SAM!"

Dobbs saw the whirlwind of dust and smoke as the missile came off the launcher—a flash of fire as the telephone pole lifted and turned toward them. Dobbs watched and then turned into the SAM. It began to move faster, the smoke billowing from it as it climbed. The first stage fell away and the SAM turned toward the flight.

Dobbs pushed the stick forward and dived at the missile, the flight right behind him. Triple-A opened up, the tracers flashing past them. Clouds of flak burst around them. Dobbs rolled to the right and hauled back on the stick, climbing out, and then rolled over again, diving toward the ground.

The flight spread out, each man moving out of position as he turned and twisted to lose the SAM missile, and to dodge the flak. The SAM followed them for a moment and then seemed to spiral off, climbing upward, toward the sun.

Dobbs climbed again, away from the alley of flak and tracers. As he straightened out, he said, "Wasp, check."

"Two."

"Three."

"Four."

Dobbs then looked at his map and the Doppler and realized they were now nearly a hundred miles off course. He turned back to the west.

All around them, there were more calls of SAM missiles and antiaircraft fire. For the moment, Dobbs was in the eye of the storm. No one was shooting at him and no MiGs were searching for him.

And then it all went to hell.

"SAM at one o'clock."

Dobbs glanced out the cockpit canopy and saw the missile. Before he could react, another was launched, and then another. He turned, diving at the SAM site, and turned again, twisting away and then climbing again, trying to fool the enemy radar.

It looked good for a moment, and then the last three missiles on the site lifted as one. The enemy commander had salvoed his weapons. The blast obscured the ground with dust and smoke.

"Coming up! Coming up!"

"To the right!"

"Hit the burners!"

One of the missiles spiraled away and detonated a half-klick behind them. Another turned with the flight and exploded behind them. Over the roar of the jet engines, Dobbs heard the detonation and felt the shock wave from it. His jet was shoved forward and downward as he fought the controls.

As his flight rolled right and left, trying to avoid the enemy missiles, with tracers slashing the air around them, and their radios crackling with MiGs, Dobbs realized that the tap points had been exaggerated. He hadn't expected to get hit for at least another ten minutes, but almost from the moment they had crossed over the North Vietnamese coast, the enemy had been on them.

Dobbs rolled, climbed nearly straight up, and then rolled over into a dive. He jinked right and left, trying to avoid the enemy missiles in abrupt maneuvers that would have flunked him out of flight school. All the while, in the back of his mind he could hear his instructor pilot telling him, "You follow flight lead and that's all you do. If he flies into the ground, there had better be another crater right beside his."

That meant that the flight was with him, maybe strung out slightly from the rapid maneuvering, but there none the less. He pulled up as another SAM turned toward them, flashed under them, and exploded in a geyser of mud and water as it slammed into the ground.

Dobbs glanced around wildly, but there were no more

missiles and no more tracers. They had flown out of the storm for a minute. He began a rapid climb back to altitude, and as he leveled off, he said, "Wasp, check."

"Two."

"Three."

"And four, except that I'm ten miles back. How about slowing it down?"

"Out of burners," said Dobbs.

As he said that, they crossed another SAM site. One of the missiles launched and flew straight up at them.

"SAM coming up."

Before Dobbs could react, the missile slammed into Wasp two, exploding, the fiery cloud engulfing the whole aircraft. Dobbs expected it to fly out, but that never happened. There was a rain of metal parts as the expanding cloud darkened and then began to dissipate. Flaming wreckage fell toward the ground.

"Two's gone," said Wasp three unnecessarily.

The flak started again, black-gray puffs of smoke close to the flight. Shrapnel rattled against Dobbs's fuselage. There was buffeting, and warning lights began to flash. Buzzers and fire warning lights came on around him. The controls became stiff, sluggish, as if their hydraulic lines had been severed. The nose dipped and Dobbs fought to bring it up again.

"SAMs," yelled someone.

Dobbs couldn't worry about them at the moment. His aircraft was beginning a slow roll to the left that he couldn't stop. He fought it using the stick and the rudders. He was aware of tracers streaking past, great glowing red orbs that suddenly had grown to the size of basketballs.

"Three's in trouble."

"SAMs!"

"Hit the burners," said Dobbs, but as he did, nothing happened. The other two planes flashed past him, suddenly flying much faster than him. That was what saved him.

SAMs lifted from another of the complexes. Dobbs saw it all as if watching it on television. The missiles, long, slender, looking just like the telephone poles that everyone claimed they did, rose from clouds of dust, leaping into the air. They turned slowly until their booster stages separated, and then they began spiraling in, following the movements of the two jets.

One of the pilots, Dobbs didn't know if it was Doyle or Augustine, tried to turn away from one missile and flew into another. There was an explosion and the plane came out, almost intact. The canopy blew off and it looked as if the pilot was going to get out, but then the jet shuddered once, like a big dog shaking off water. There was a cloud of black smoke from the engine and the jet exploded. There was no chute. The pilot hadn't gotten out.

The pilot of the other plane turned twice and dived for the ground, a missile turning with him. He pulled around, then climbed and dived, and the missile went spinning off on its own.

A second came at him and exploded down and away, the edge of the smoke just touching the jet. It flipped the jet over, but the pilot, either Augustine or Doyle, righted it and the canopy popped. The jet, trailing smoke, climbed higher. Flames burst out along the underside of the jet, covering its belly and trying to spread to the wings.

*"Get out!"* yelled Dobbs.

Just as he spoke, the pilot hit the ejector and was blown clear of the plane. The chute opened beautifully, and although some of the North Vietnamese gunners were shooting at him, the tracers seemed to be wide of the mark. The pilot's beeper, an emergency radio attached to the parachute, began to bark, signaling all that he was out of his aircraft and heading toward the ground.

Dobbs was going to begin the procedure to get air-sea rescue in. They needed the slower-moving A-1E Skyraiders and the HH-53 helicopters. This close to the coast, this far from Hanoi, they had a real shot at getting the pilot out.

But then, with only one aircraft still around, all the enemy gunners turned their attention to Dobbs. The flak became thicker, as he turned to circle the downed pilot. Streams of tracers ripped into the sky, some of them punching through the wings and fuselage of his aircraft. He could feel them as they tore the thin metal skin and destroyed the avionics, the wiring, the control cables. More buzzers screamed and more warning lights flashed.

Dobbs tried to turn, to begin a run to the South China Sea. If he could get there, the helicopters would be over him before he could hit the water. In North Vietnam, it was much harder to get downed crewmen out.

He didn't want to leave his downed friend, but there was nothing he could do. To stay on station would mean that he would soon be on the ground with him. The man had a survival radio which he could use to contact the rescue crews and other flight crews. Dobbs could accomplish nothing by remaining.

Then the fire that had been concealed under the belly of his fighter began to creep up the sides. He could see the flames, now, blowing back along the fuselage. Turning in his seat, he could see the long, looping trail of black smoke that marked his path through the North Vietnamese sky.

The enemy fire grew thicker, as if they sensed that the plane was about to die. They followed it, sending up walls of lead. Dobbs dodged through it as the warnings kept wailing and the lights kept flashing. Heat and then smoke began to fill the cockpit. Dobbs whispered to himself, asking for another two minutes, another two minutes. Just enough time to get over the South China Sea.

On the horizon, he saw the first thin line that marked the water, his sanctuary. Only moments away. And then the airplane rolled over as the last of the control cables were severed. Fire had burned away part of the airfoils and the tail. The plane was no longer controllable, and Dobbs knew that he was going to have to get out.

He reached down and blasted the canopy free. As the fresh air swirled in the cockpit of death, blowing away the smoke, Dobbs thought that his premonition had been a day early. It had been yesterday that he was supposed to die. He had known it yesterday. Today, the mission had been just another thrown together at the last minute. He hadn't even had time to worry about it because it had been designed so quickly.

With the aircraft losing altitude rapidly, there was

nothing more for him to do. He wouldn't reach the safety of the South China Sea, but that didn't matter. He was close enough to walk to the beach if he had to. It was only a matter of days. If that was necessary.

As he tried to eject, the plane shuddered once, as if suddenly cold. There was a thud, like he had flown through some kind of barrier, and then the plane exploded, disintegrating in the air. Dobbs never knew what hit him.

It was after dark when Taylor finally returned to the Gunfighter's Club. Linda had ridden in the cab to the base with him and then had run on ahead, afraid of being fired for being more than two hours late. Taylor had not wanted to run. He had wanted to stroll along, taking in the sights, the sounds, the odors around him. He had wanted the chance to enjoy himself for his last few hours of freedom, and he had wanted to watch the Air Force personnel working. Enlisted men cleaning the grounds around the barracks, MPs armed with M-16s watching the gates, the men in jeeps and trucks heading to their posts. A military base in action.

And in front of him, a klick away, was the flight line. There was the continuous roar of jet engines as fighters took off for missions over South Vietnam. Multiple-engine jets, transports, were taking men to R and R spots or rotating them out of the hellhole of South Vietnam. And propeller-driven airplanes, both transports and fighters, were leaving for missions in South Vietnam. Of course, there was the ever-present popping of rotorblades as helicopters worked the area.

All of it had a relaxing effect on Taylor. Like normal

missions flown out of every base in the world, these were nothing that unusual. Just men flying airplanes as men did the world over. The only real difference here was that the enemy sometimes shot at you, but if you weren't detailed for a mission north of the DMZ, the odds were with you all the way.

He walked to the club, expecting to find Dobbs and Hopper waiting for him, already pleasantly drunk after a day in Saigon. Maybe they'd eat dinner and maybe they'd drink it.

The interior of the club was smoke-filled and loud. Rock and roll was blaring and a group of Army helicopter pilots was arguing with a group of Air Force pilots. One side was claiming the other didn't see any real action. The real danger was close to the ground, outside the envelope flown by the Air Force. That was countered by claiming the real danger was up north, above the DMZ, off limits to the Army.

Taylor stopped by the door, saw Linda was already working, but couldn't find either Dobbs or Hopper. He watched the two groups of pilots continue to argue, some of it becoming heated. One man shoved his face close to the man near him and shouted at him, the words lost in the rumble from the speakers, and the rock and roll. He wondered how long it would be before someone threw a punch and started a fight. That was usually how these things ended.

Before he could move, he felt a hand on his shoulder. Thinking it was either Hopper or Dobbs, he turned and was surprised to find Ott standing there, looking grim and pale.

"There you are," said Ott.

"Yes," shouted Taylor, over the music and the noise. "Here I am."

"Let's get out of here," said Ott.

"There a problem?"

"We've had some bad news," said Ott. He turned and began to move through the door.

"Oh shit," said Taylor, suddenly weak. He knew what was coming without being told. Knew as surely as if he had read about it. "No," he said, staring right at Ott, and then added, "Oh shit."

# EIGHT

OSBORNE had finished the afternoon route package and was on his way to the debriefing when Platte found him. He said, "You've got to come with me," and then headed for the waiting staff car.

Osborne caught him at the door and said, "I really should make the debriefing, and I'd like a chance to get rid of my flight gear."

"Get in," said Platte. He opened the rear door and climbed into the backseat.

When Osborne joined him, Platte said, "We've got a major problem going down."

The driver started the engine and turned up the air conditioner to high. Over the roar of the fan, Platte asked, "How soon will you be ready to deploy?"

"Deploy?" asked Osborne, chuckling. "Deploy where?"

"Vietnam."

"Are you serious?"

Platte looked out the window as the flight line disappeared behind them. He pulled a handkerchief from his pocket and mopped his face, trying to buy some time so that he didn't have to answer the question, but the tactic didn't work.

"Listen, the North Vietnamese have been deploying their SAMs for several months, and now they're using them. Firing them at our planes. Firing hundreds of them in the last two days. We've got to do something."

"Sure," agreed Osborne, "but the answer is not deploying us before we're ready. That's not the answer to the North Vietnamese problem."

"What more is needed?" asked Platte.

To Osborne, the list seemed to be endless, from more intelligence and more briefings on the Soviet-built SA-2 SAM and the triple-A defenses around those sites, to more time to familiarize themselves with the aircraft and the new equipment. No one had thought about tactics or the best method to suppress the SAMs.

"We still don't know if this is going to work," said Osborne. "The theories on some of it are still a little shaky, and I don't want to hit a combat environment until we've had a chance to work out some of the problems."

"True enough," said Platte, "but I'm afraid that the dictates of the war demand that we push ahead."

"We're not ready," said Osborne.

The car slowed and then turned. As it picked up speed, Platte said, "I'm afraid that this really isn't a matter for discussion. The orders have been cut."

Osborne fell back in the seat and stared upward at the dome light, as if looking for divine inspiration. "I've sat through two briefings here, explaining the SADS system. It operates on the principle that this is the way the Soviet-built Fan Song and the Fire Can radars work. Our detectors in the aircraft are geared to that. Geared to the SADS."

"What's the point?"

"The point is that if the first theory is wrong, and the SADS do not simulate the Soviet-built radars, then we're going to be flying blind."

"Technicians in Vietnam are working the problem," said Platte. "We've ECM aircraft over the South China Sea searching for the signals and radio traffic of the North Vietnamese. If we don't have the frequencies now, we will soon. Minor adjustments can be made."

"But we're not ready," said Osborne. "We haven't worked out the tactics, we aren't completely familiar with the equipment, and the backseaters need more training on the equipment capabilities."

Platte grinned at that. "Your words move me to tears, but there isn't one thing you've said that will change anyone's mind, given the situation in Vietnam."

Now Osborne found himself sweating heavily, even in the frigid car. He touched the sleeve of his flight suit to his forehead and wished that he was somewhere else.

They pulled into a parking lot in front of a large, brick building. There was a flagpole in front of it, flowers under the windows, and a large, landscaped lawn. Platte opened the door, got out, and waited for Osborne.

As soon as Osborne was out, Platte waved him toward the double doors. They walked up the sidewalk and entered the building. Like the car, the interior was cold, but Osborne was still sweating.

As they walked down the hallway, the walls lined with pictures of fighters from the First World War to the current crop in Vietnam, Platte was talking. "Just listen to what's being said and remember that there is nothing you can do about it now. Everyone is ready to go."

They passed a display case filled with models of airplanes. Old ones and new ones and a few that were experimental. The green tile of the floor gave way to a thick blue carpet, and Osborne knew that the man who had the office at the end of the hall was a general who probably commanded a large unit.

They reached a wooden door that was fancier than all those they had passed. The knob was brass that had to have been polished daily. Osborne could see the traces of Brasso where the man who had polished it had failed to wipe it all away.

A brass plaque in the center of the door at eye level read simply, LT GEN CLARENCE C. AUGUSTINE.

They entered the office and found it almost deserted. There were two desks, one for the civilian secretary and one for the general's aide. There were bookcases along one wall, chairs for visitors against another, and a bank of windows, the curtains drawn, on the third.

Osborne stopped in his tracks when he saw the secretary. A young woman with long black hair, she was crying. She held a handkerchief to her face, but it didn't conceal the tears. She didn't bother to glance at either of the men.

"What's the deal here?" asked Platte.

The woman looked up, surprised by the two men. She wiped her eyes and said, "The general just got word that his son is missing in action over North Vietnam."

"Oh, shit," said Osborne. He knew what missing in action meant in most cases. The man was dead and they were waiting for confirmation of the identification. It was a dodge they used to keep from notifying a family that someone had been killed and then finding out he hadn't been.

"What happened?" asked Platte.

"No one knows," said the woman. She sniffed and added. "They just said that his flight ran into heavy fire and disappeared. No one knows for sure."

"We've an appointment with the general," said Platte.

"He's not seeing anyone today."

Osborne turned to go, but Platte restrained him with a hand to his forearm. "I know it's bad timing, but please let the general know that we're here. I think he'll want to see us."

"I don't know. . ."

"Please," said Platte. "Let him decide the matter."

The door to the general's office opened, and a man stepped out. His face was set in hard lines, his lips pressed together firmly. He was a young man with pilot's wings above his pocket. He might have been twenty-two or twenty-three.

"Colonel Platte?"

"Yes."

"General Augustine has just received some very bad news . . ."

"We heard."

"Yes sir. Anyway, if you'd give him a few minutes, he'd appreciate it. Then he'll be ready to see you."

"We could come back later," said Platte, "if that would be convenient."

"No, sir. Please be seated."

Platte shrugged and sat down as the aide disappeared again.

"I don't like this," said Osborne.

"Nothing we can do about it," said Platte. "The general wants us to wait, so we have to wait."

"That's not what I meant," said Osborne. "If the general feels up to seeing us, that's his business. What I don't like is having the training schedule curtailed in this fashion. I think it makes more sense for us to stay here and develop the mission package so that it can be used effectively in Vietnam. In the long run, that is the smart move."

Platte glanced at the secretary who got up and moved to the door, disappearing into the corridor. As she departed, Platte turned and said, "You've been bitching about this since we got into the car. What the hell is wrong?"

"Okay," said Osborne, feeling his blood boil. "What's wrong? This is so typical of the military. We have a theory, partially proven on ranges, that in the next few days we're suddenly going to try in Vietnam. Makes no difference that there are people who worry that we might have missed something vital in the intelligence briefings. Makes no difference that nothing like this has been tried yet. The idea works fine on paper so it'll work fine in the field."

"You have doubts," said Platte sarcastically.

"I have doubts," said Osborne, "because it's my butt that's going to be hanging out over North Vietnam. Not yours or the bureaucrats in Washington."

"You still haven't said anything specific," said Platte.

"Specific? How about no one knowing whether or not this is going to work? We think we've got the frequencies used by the Soviets. We think we can intercept the signals. We think that the signal strength is enough to give us a launch detection. We think we can get indications of direction and distance to the site. That's what we think. But we don't know. We lose one link in that chain and everything comes apart."

"I believe the theory is a little more sound than that," countered Platte.

"Sound enough that you'll hang your butt out over North Vietnam?"

"Sometimes the dictates of the situation are such that there is no choice one way or the other."

"I just wish we knew if this damned thing is going to work, or if we're all going to come tumbling out of the sky."

Platte shrugged and said, "There is always an element of risk when new systems are developed."

"And it's always someone else who has to take the risks," Osborne shot back.

"That's not totally fair, Major."

Osborne stared at the man for a moment and then said, "You're right. I'm sorry. It wasn't your decision to send us in already. I should confine my concerns to the proper channels."

"Well, there is nothing we can do about it now," said

Platte. "All we can do is sit here and wait for the general to let us know if it's a go or not."

There didn't seem to be anything to say to that, so Osborne sat there quietly, and waited. Platte picked up a copy of a magazine and flipped through it. He worked from the back to the front and then tossed it to the table.

The aide returned finally and came over to them. He stood there for a moment and then said, "The general will see you now. He has lost his only son today..."

"He get any more news?" asked Platte.

"No, sir. He's been in touch with Tan Son Nhut, but right now they don't seem to know what has happened. Just that he is missing, but given the distances and fuel capacities, he has to be down over North Vietnam. There have been some reports that there are men on the ground and that rescue operations are under way, but no one knows who's on the ground and who's not."

"How is the general?" asked Osborne.

"Well, sir, how would you feel if someone had told you that your son was missing over Vietnam?"

"Yeah," said Osborne. "I'm surprised he still wants to see us."

"I think he feels that you'll have the opportunity to get even for him and his son, and right now that's what he wants the most."

An hour later, Osborne was in a room with the other pilots and the ground crews. He sat on a table while Platte stood at the rear leaning against the wall. Everyone was talking at once until Osborne started staring at them to silence them.

"We're on alert for Vietnam," said Osborne without

preamble, when he had their attention. "The situation there is getting so bad that they want us in Vietnam as quickly as possible."

"What's this on alert mean?"

Osborne looked at Kenyon and said, "It means we've got maybe two days to get ready. Maybe not. If there is anything you need to do before you go to Vietnam for a year, you'd better get it done now."

"You mean like getting laid?" asked Froiseth, turning to the others to see if they appreciated his fine analysis of the situation.

There was a bark of laughter. Osborne smiled and then said, "I would think that there would be other things that have to be done first. Oh, for those of you who are married, I'm afraid that you won't be able to give your destination to your wives until after we've arrived."

"Why's that?" asked Benning.

Osborne shrugged. "Somebody got bitten by the security bug, I guess. Don't want to telegraph the punch." He held up his hands to stop the protest. "It makes no sense to me either, but those are the orders."

"How we going to get there?" asked Dallas.

"Pilots and electronic warfare officers will fly out in the five aircraft currently equipped with the new systems. Ground crew and support gear will be loaded on a C-141 and flown into Tan Son Nhut. Right now the scheduling is a little shaky, so I can't give you times."

"What are we going to have to take with us?"

Osborne shrugged. "I've a list here. Everything we need will be available in Vietnam. We'll be issued uniforms, fatigues, and such once we arrive in-country."

"Christ," snapped one of the members of the ground crew. "I don't want to do this."

Osborne looked toward him. He was an old master sergeant, forty, forty-five years old, with graying hair and a deeply lined face.

"I would have thought that you would have learned long ago to never volunteer for anything," said Osborne.

"Kee-rist, sir, they told me I'd have the chance to work on the leading edge of a new technology and to get some TDY pay in Florida. No one said anything about Vietnam."

"George," interrupted one of the other sergeants, "when was the last time the Air Force ever gave anyone a good deal? You should've known."

"But, Kee-rist. Vietnam."

"Anything else?" asked Osborne.

The men were all quiet, and Osborne said, "All right. That's it for now. We'll check in at eight tomorrow and see if we have orders. If not, you'll have the day to prepare and another check-in at two. If no one wants to bitch about this anymore, you're released."

As the men filed out of the room, Kenyon came forward and asked. "This going to be a full-year tour in Vietnam?"

Osborne shrugged. "I imagine so."

"I thought there were regulations against them doing this to people. We're on TDY here, and suddenly we're on change of station to Vietnam. They can't force us into a PCS move."

Osborne had to laugh. "I think you'll find they can do anything they want. There will be some obscure regulation that let's them do it. And I don't think the year tour in Vietnam qualifies as a permanent change of station."

"Still," said Kenyon.

"Lieutenant," said Platte, moving forward, "I think you'll find that since you volunteered for this assignment in the blind, as it were, that you've agreed to do what has to be done to complete it. In other words, you're screwed, blued, and tattooed."

"Yes, sir."

"And if you were to call a congressman to complain," continued Platte, "I think you'd find that you suddenly had TDY orders to Vietnam instead of the PCS orders. They can send you TDY anywhere they want as long as they can prove critical job description. And since there are no other people trained in the Wild Weasel mission, your job description is critical. Nothing you can do about it."

"At least I'd pick up the extra TDY money."

"Yes," agreed Platte, "but you'd have a rough time making captain when the time comes. The Air Force doesn't forget those who have made waves."

"Is that a threat?" asked Kenyon.

"Sit down, Lieutenant," said Platte. "Sit down, and let's not let our emotions get away from us here."

Kenyon stared at Platte and then pulled a chair out and sat down. He didn't say a word.

"Lieutenant, I'm going to explain the facts of life to you, and save you some time and a great deal of trouble, in the event that you want a military career."

"Go ahead."

"First, if you interest a congressman in your career by making waves, your 201 file will be flagged with a congressional-influence notation. Right there you're a marked man, and anything that anyone can do to you will be done."

"Great . . ."

"And, second, you'll have to go to Vietnam anyway. It's a no-win situation. You just have to live with it. Make waves about it and it's you who will suffer in the long run. I can't stress that point enough."

"Great . . ."

Platte said, "If there is anything I can do for you between now and your departure, let me know."

"Yeah. Thanks," said Kenyon, not sounding as if he meant it. He got up and left the briefing room without looking back.

"Kid's got a lot to learn about the Air Force and the workings of the military," said Platte, as Kenyon disappeared from sight.

"I hope he gets the chance," said Osborne.

Osborne returned to his quarters in the VOQ. It was a Spartan room with a bed that was little more than a cot, a single chair, and a narrow desk that had most of the top taken up by a black-and-white TV set. There was a refrigerator stuck in one corner, but it didn't work and, from the dust on it, probably hadn't worked in a year or more. The floor was bare except for a small rug by the bed. There were venetian blinds on the window but no curtains, and if he wanted to use the phone, he had to walk down the hallway.

Packing took almost no time. He hadn't brought much, and he knew that his white underwear would be replaced with olive drab in Vietnam. Once in-country he would get OD towels and washcloths and be given jungle fatigues. The only thing he had to take with him was his flight gear and any civilian clothes he might want.

Once he had everything stuffed into the single suitcase he used because he hated the duffel bags that the military was so fond of, he sat down in the chair and stared at the darkened screen of the TV.

He didn't know what to expect. Too young to have flown in Korea, and having met dozens of pilots who had, he didn't know if they were handing him a line, or if combat was as rough as they made it sound. He'd been through the various schools designed to teach him what he needed to know, he'd seen the gun-camera films taken during Korea and some of the new stuff from Vietnam, but he'd never experienced aerial combat for himself. Simulated missions just weren't the same precisely because they were simulated. Everyone knew that a mistake probably wouldn't kill. The enemy was actually friends who took on the role of enemy for the day.

It just wasn't the same.

And now he was going into war, not prepared as well as he should have been, where people would be shooting at him for real. A mistake that would cause an instructor or a commander to yell could now be fatal. The enemy would be shooting at him with real bullets, and failure could mean death, not just a failing grade in the class.

Of course, it would be just as it had always been for him. The night before any move to a new base, or a new school, he was worried, afraid, but once he was involved in it, he found it less frightening. It was the unknown that scared him. He knew, deep in his gut, that he would perform well because he always did. He would sit in the cockpit and do the job no matter what was going on around him. All he had to do was remember his training and do his job and not worry about anything else. Training was everything.

There was a knock at his door, then. Osborne got up and walked over, opening it.

"You Osborne?" asked the young man dressed only in jockey shorts. Tight jockey shorts.

"Yeah."

"Call for you."

Osborne walked down the hall and grabbed the receiver. "Osborne."

"This is Colonel Platte. You are now officially alerted with a takeoff time of 0900 tomorrow. Alert your people."

"Ground crews?"

"Ranking sergeant has been notified and given the responsibility to gather everyone else for a takeoff at 1100 hours tomorrow. It's not something that you need to worry about. You just have to get your people alerted, and get your personal gear to the flight line for the C-141. Briefings will begin at 0615. Questions?"

Osborne couldn't think of anything that he wanted to know. Platte had given him everything with the words that they were going in the morning.

"Nothing."

"Then alert your people."

"Yessir."

"And good luck, Major. I know they've thrown you a curve on this one, but I think it'll work out for you."

"Thank you." Osborne hung up the phone and stood

staring at it for a moment. He was numb now, unsure how he felt. He had known it was coming, but hadn't expected it quite so quickly. If someone had asked him to describe his thoughts, his feelings, he wouldn't have been able to do it.

He turned and walked back toward his room, trying to figure out his first move. Obviously he would have to walk over to the club and tell the men there that they had gotten the word. Already they had gotten the word. Then he could send them out to find the others, and post a note on the bulletin board. No, not on the bulletin board, because that would tell anyone who happened to look at it that the orders had come through. It was just that type of thinking that compromised missions. Tomorrow he would have to walk by every room and wake up all the pilots.

He collapsed into the chair and stared at the TV screen. All he could think was, *Jesus Christ, they're really going to send us.*

# NINE

TAYLOR sat in the small office and was aware of everything around him. Acutely aware. The stench from the engines of the fighters and transports operating on the airfield, the heat and humidity, and the sweat dripping down his body. He was also aware that while he'd been having a good time with Linda, watching her take off her clothes, lying in bed with her, fucking his brains out, the members of his flight, his friends, had been dying over North Vietnam.

The emotions bubbled through him, setting his teeth on edge. He wanted to throw something, hit something. He pounded his fist against the desk, and it threatened to collapse.

The ironic thing was that no one blamed him. They congratulated him on getting out of it by not hanging around. No one had told him he had to stay close to the squadron area, and a few minutes in Saigon, hopping bars, listening to music, and chasing women was a diversion that they all sought. Without a specific assignment, he was authorized to take off for the day. He'd done nothing wrong.

He stood up and walked around the desk and sat down again. "If I did nothing wrong," he said out loud, "why do I feel I've betrayed everyone?"

Trying to occupy his mind, he looked at the frag and saw that theirs had been an add-on mission, one that they couldn't plan for. That was why it had been thrown together with the pilots who were still available, those who had decided to sleep in and to hang around completing the paperwork that he had been dodging.

"Proving," he said to himself, "that no good deed goes unpunished."

The door opened and Ott entered. Without a word he dropped into the folding metal chair sitting in front of the desk. He sat there for a moment, quietly, and then asked, "Are you okay?"

"I'm just ginger peachy."

"Okay," said Ott, "let's talk about this for a moment."

"There's no need," snapped Taylor. "I know all the arguments by heart and don't want to hear them again. It wasn't my fault. I didn't send them out. I was clever in getting off the base before the frag hit."

"There you go," said Ott.

"And I believe it, too," said Taylor.

"All right," said Ott, "I know you won't accept anyone's word on this. Just remember one thing—you didn't run out on your friends and fellows. It wasn't like Lord Jim, who had the chance to do something brave but didn't. You didn't have the chance to get into the fight today. Yesterday you did, and I haven't seen any evidence of cowardice in your performance up to this point."

Taylor was smart enough to know that everyone who had faced death or flown over North Vietnam had been scared. Each had felt the panic as the first rounds came up at him, or as the first SAM was launched. But each had gone on, flying through the clouds of flak and passing the SAM sites, on to the target. Taylor wasn't sure if it was because each man had conquered his fear or if it was just that there was no way to run. All he knew was that each man went on, in the face of the danger, without the question of bravery ever surfacing.

And he was secure in the knowledge that he was no coward. As the flight leader, he could have aborted the hairy missions, the ones that were flown between the cloud decks, or under them, as the enemy fired volleys up at the jets. Mission requirements only dictated that he look at the target, not necessarily attack it. He could have aborted the hairy missions to come back some other time, but he'd never exercised that option. He'd pressed on in the face of the danger.

No, he wasn't a coward. So that meant his feelings, his emotions, were about something else, about letting his friends and colleagues down when they needed him most.

"What's the plan now?" asked Taylor, to hide his emotions.

"With four aircraft gone and four pilots lost, we've received a reduced mission package for the time being.

Until we can find replacements for the people and the equipment, that is. It's no reflection on you."

"Uh-huh," said Taylor. The question was, what was going to happen to him now that his flight had been wiped away.

"Once we have the replacements, we'll get you back into the air. Right now, I think you should take some time off. Maybe put in for R and R."

"No, sir," said Taylor. "That's the last thing I need. I need to get into the air."

"Then a couple of days. In-country R and R. Hang out in Saigon, live in one of the hotels, eat at the restaurants. Take it easy."

"Your talking like I was involved in this. Like I've just come back from the mission."

Ott shook his head and said, "I know how this can affect a man's performance. I've seen it before. You've nothing to be ashamed of, but you feel that you let your friends down. You should have been there and should have died with them."

Taylor started to speak, but Ott wouldn't let him. "That's bullshit. The mission came late and you didn't know about it. You weren't available and others were. Your good fortune. Now, you can let that eat at you and destroy you, or you can figure that your time just wasn't up. It wasn't time for you to die . . ."

"But . . ."

Ott held up a hand. "I know a helicopter pilot, guy in the Crusaders, I think. Told me he'd been flying a helicopter all day. They do preflights, check the equipment just like we do. He'd checked the rotor head before takeoff. After they landed, he was making the postflight and part of the rotor assembly came apart in his hand. If it had happened in flight, the aircraft would have crashed, probably killing everyone on board. It held together just long enough."

"What's the point?"

"You can't second-guess your second chances. You just take them and run with them, happy that you've got them." Ott grinned and said, "Besides, you don't know, maybe the guys who died are the lucky ones."

"How the hell can you say that?"

Ott shrugged and said, "We don't know what happens afterward. If we did, and it was all that the chaplains tell us it is, we'd all kill ourselves now to get out of this life. Think about that. We're told about our reward when this life is ended, but we're all afraid of that reward. We hang on here."

"Christ," said Taylor, "that's the dumbest thing I've ever heard."

Now Ott nodded. "Maybe so. It's just something that I sometimes think about. Anyway, I want you to take some time off. Put some distance between today and you. Get yourself drunk or laid or whatever."

"Yes, sir," said Taylor.

Ott stood up and wiped a hand across his face. "Paperwork will wait."

"Notifications?"

"Have been made. I'll wait about a week and then write letters to the families." Ott moved to the door and stopped. "I never know whether the families want the damned letters or not. There's nothing I can tell them except that their son or husband or father was a good soldier and died fighting for something he believed in."

"Maybe that's enough," said Taylor. "Just knowing that he was doing his job."

"Yeah, maybe."

Taylor stood up and stretched. He felt better having talked to Ott. He watched the other officer walk out, his shoulders slumped as he thought about the burden of the letters that he had to write.

Taylor caught up with him in the hallway and asked, "Mind if I write the letters?"

"It's something that I should do," said Ott halfheartedly.

"Yes, sir, but the men were in my flight, or rather it was my flight that had drawn the mission. I'd feel better if you'd let me write them."

"Fine," said Ott. "Let me see a draft before they're mailed out."

"Yes, sir."

Taylor returned to his office and stared at the walls for a moment, thinking about everything that had been said. He knew, deep down, that Ott was right about everything, from why he shouldn't blame himself to why he should take a couple of days off to relax. It wasn't as if he'd gotten drunk and couldn't fly the mission because of alcohol. He was blameless and everyone knew it.

And that was the key. No one blamed him. They saw it as an act of fate. If he'd been around, he could have flown, but since he was not, he couldn't. No one had known that the mission was coming.

Taylor got up and moved to the door again. He snapped off the lights and left. Outside, there was a soft breeze from the east, cooling things off. It was the first time since he'd been in Vietnam that he remembered a cool breeze coming from anywhere. A nice night, good weather, and if it hadn't been for the glow of the lights of Saigon, he could have seen the stars clearly.

He walked out toward the flight line and stopped at the eight-foot-high chain-link fence that surrounded the airfield proper. He stood there for a moment, watching the airplanes taking off. Their landing lights blazing and their navigation lights blinking, the jets roared down the runway and lifted. Then there was the glow from their engines as the planes climbed out, heading for missions over South Vietnam.

Finally he turned and walked toward the Gunfighter's Club. As he approached, he heard the rock and roll and stopped for a second. There was something about it that depressed him, and he didn't know what it was. Something about going to the club where only a few days earlier he'd been buying drinks for Dobbs and Hopper and the others. Now they were dead in North Vietnam, their bodies probably no more than bits and pieces for the scavengers.

"Lovely thought," he said to himself. And then figured that it didn't matter to Dobbs or Hopper or the other two.

He entered the club, watched the people as they circulated, and then moved down toward a table. He found a couple of men that he knew and joined them without asking. When a waitress passed close, he waved at her and yelled, "Beer."

There were those who insisted they could taste the difference in various beers, and Taylor was sure that some people could. But that made no difference to him, because he couldn't. A beer was a beer.

As the waitress reappeared with the bottle, he saw Linda working. She had changed into a very short skirt and a tight blouse that was now sweat-soaked with the heat in the club. Her hair hung straight down, as if she had just gotten out of the shower.

Taylor took his beer and shouldered his way through the crowd of men who were shouting and whistling at the girl who was dancing and refusing to take off any of her clothes. Taylor knew that it was part of the act. Reluctantly, she would shed one garment after another until she was naked, and then would work the crowd for tips, making as much as a hundred dollars for the ten-minute show.

Taylor wasn't sure why he was suddenly chasing Linda through the Gunfighter's Club. While he had been with her, his friends had been dying, but that hadn't been her fault. Ott had made sure Taylor didn't think it was his fault. It was one of those things that happened in war. The wrong man in the wrong place at the wrong time. Taylor had lucked into being in the right place at the right time. Because of all that, he wanted to see Linda again.

Taylor caught up with her as she finished delivering a round of beers to a table of Navy pilots. He leaned close to her. "How long do you have to work?"

She glanced at him, smiled, and said, "To one o'clock."

"Can you get out of here earlier?"

"Why?"

Taylor shrugged and said, "Because I want to be with

you for the night. Because it's been a lousy evening, and I want to forget about it."

"I make one hundred dollar if I stay. I make big tips."

Taylor stood up straight and looked at the small woman. Studied her closely and felt his desire grow. But just for her. He could have gone down to Tu Do Street and found a hooker who would have become whoever he wanted her to be. He could have found a hooker who would cater to his every whim, becoming his sexual slave, if he'd had the money to pay for it.

But that was not what he wanted. He needed someone he knew, even if the relationship had only started that morning. They had shared something earlier. Theirs was a relationship that was based on something other than his being able to pay for it. Except now she was asking for him to pay for it.

"I don't have that kind of money," he said, knowing that she knew he did.

"You wait until I finish."

Taylor didn't want to do that either. He wanted to get out of there now. Away from the men who had forgotten about everything except drink and women. They had reduced the war, at that moment, to a naked woman and a filled glass.

Taylor was almost ready to tell her that he would make up her tips if she would come with him. But then she looked up and said, "You wait. I come."

Taylor stood there as she headed toward the bar, detoured, and disappeared into one of the back rooms. He moved toward the bar and waited, sipping the beer and trying not to hear the blaring music or the shouting men. He watched the door, waiting for her and trying to think about her and what they would do. His mind kept returning to the men who had died that day.

He finished the beer as Linda returned. She was dressed differently now. The skirt was longer and the blouse not nearly so tight.

"Where we go?"

"Downtown," said Taylor. He wanted to find a hotel that had hot and cold running water, all-night electricity, and air-conditioning. He wanted something comfortable and clean and quiet. A place to hide.

They left the club, walked to the gate, and stood there waiting as the traffic swirled around them. A taxi, an old Ford that had been painted a dozen different colors by a dozen different owners, dived out of the flow of traffic and squealed to a halt near them.

"You want ride?" the driver yelled.

Taylor grabbed the rear handle and opened the door. Once they were inside, Taylor told the driver to take them downtown, to the Continental Hotel, the one where all the reporters and civilians stayed. A full-service hotel, it offered everything that any good, modern hotel offered. The war hadn't adversely affected the quality of its service.

It didn't take long to get there. They drove down streets that were brightly lighted. People—soldiers in civilian clothes, locals in their traditional garb, and soldiers in uniform—circulated on the street. In one semi-dark alley, Taylor saw a man, his pants around his ankles, leaning against a girl who had her bare legs wrapped around his waist. It was obvious what they were doing, and Taylor found himself fascinated by the sight. Maybe because they didn't care if anyone saw them, or maybe because he'd never seen people doing it in public like that. At least not people who weren't being paid to perform.

Finally the taxi reached the front door of the hotel. Taylor paid off the driver and hurried into the lobby, a cavernous place with huge marble pillars and a gym-sized floor. There were chairs and sofas scattered around, most of them filled with people. There were uniformed bellmen who watched Taylor as he entered the hotel with Linda beside him.

Checking in took no time, and he paid cash for the first night. Since neither of them had luggage, not an unusual occurrence in wartime Saigon, they didn't need the services of the bellmen. One of the bellmen watched them cross the lobby, looking like someone had locked him out of the candy store.

They took the elevator to the sixth floor, and Taylor found his way to the room, unlocking the door. As he did, he heard the unmistakable sounds of two people having a good time in the next room. The woman was grunting in time to the squeaking of the bed, and the man was shouting encouragement to her.

"What the hell is going on around here?" asked Taylor.

"What do you mean?"

Taylor glanced at Linda and shook his head. He pushed the door open and let her enter in front of him. As he closed the door and locked it, she took off her blouse without a word to him or from him. When he turned, she came to him, her arms out. She jumped up and wrapped her legs around him, just as the hooker had done with the man in the street. She began to kiss his face, head, and neck, as if he were a lover she hadn't seen in several months.

Taylor was going to tell her they should relax for a moment, but then it was too late. She was trying to get his shirt unbuttoned. She put her feet on the floor and began fumbling with the buckle of his pants.

He pushed her hands away and said, "Here, let me do that."

And a moment later she was dragging him across the room to the bed, where they both collapsed, trying to get the other's clothes off in record time.

It was too late to talk.

# TEN

OSBORNE was awake most of the night. There was light bleeding into his room from the outside. Bands of light on the ceiling that he stared at as he tried to sleep. He'd tried everything he could think of, from watching a boring movie about romance on a Broadway stage, on the TV, to reading a news magazine left in the room by the last occupant. He tried relaxing himself, starting with his toes and working his way upward, but that had failed, just as everything else had failed. A deployment to Vietnam with a weapons system and tactics that hadn't been tested was guaranteed to keep anyone awake.

Finally, realizing that he wasn't going to be able to sleep, he got up and turned on the lights. He checked his suitcase, making sure that he was leaving nothing behind. He went into the bathroom, which connected to another room so that he shared it with another officer, and took a shower. He shaved and brushed his teeth and returned to his room. He stuffed his shaving kit into his suitcase and sat down at the desk.

He pulled a yellow legal pad out and started to make notes about the Wild Weasel missions. He figured that, since no one had ever tried the new system in combat, and because he had flown a number of simulated missions, he knew as much about it as anyone. He wanted to explain, in writing, what he feared would be the failure of the upcoming mission. He started with the lack of adequate training time, and continued through to the fact that no one was really sure how the SAMs and their co-located triple-A defenses worked. There was a great deal of speculation, and there were a number of intelligence reports that made claims, but none of it was documented.

That seemed to work. Start writing something, anything, and Osborne got tired. He glanced over the two pages of notes, then put his pencil down. He moved to the bed and lay down, thinking he would just rest for a moment.

The alarm clock woke him up a couple of hours later. Osborne stood, stretched, and said, "Isn't that the way." Try to sleep and can't, then give up and drop right off.

But the couple of hours was all that he needed. He felt good as he left the room and headed over to the club for breakfast. In flight school, before the first flight he'd ever taken, the instructor had told him, told the class, to eat a light breakfast. Avoid heavy foods that lay in the stomach, because that could create airsickness.

After a few days, as the students got used to flying

every day, they started eating everything in sight. Eggs, fried in thick grease, sausage, bacon, oatmeal, toast, coffee, and pancakes. It didn't matter, because they were all so busy learning to fly that they didn't have time to get sick.

Now, as he sat down to eat, he knew that it was all a matter of not making himself sick. Riding in the back of a jet airliner sometimes made his stomach queasy. Flying a jet never bothered him. Osborne ordered a huge breakfast.

As he sat there, the other pilots and the backseaters strolled in, alone or in groups of two or three. They pulled a table over so that all ten of them could eat together.

Kenyon, looking slightly gray, as if he hadn't slept at all, dropped into a chair next to Osborne and asked, "Is this trip really necessary?"

"I don't think so," said Osborne, "but then we have orders, so we'll have to go."

After sitting for a minute or so, as if resting, the men stood and moved to the buffet. All of them, knowing that they had a long day and a long flight in front of them, piled their plates high with food.

When everyone was seated again, Osborne noticed that they were quiet. It wasn't just a question of it being early in the morning with the men tired, but the knowledge of what was going to happen. In a couple of hours they would be taking off on a flight that would take them to Vietnam.

"I figure that we'll have one, maybe two layovers before we hit South Vietnam," said Osborne. "Then probably a week of orientation flights, till we get accustomed to the climate."

"Can't be any worse than the weather here."

"Except no one is shooting at you here," said Kenyon.

"That's the thing that bothers me the most," said Daniels. "We're being thrown into this thing very quickly."

"Not much that we can do about it now," said Kenyon, remembering his discussion with Platte the night before.

Tim Casey, one of the EWOs, sat there quietly for a minute and then said, "If we've got the frequencies right, and the various instruments calibrated right, we know everything that we have to know."

"And if they're wrong," said Daniels, "then we're up shit creek without a spoon."

"Gentlemen," said Osborne, "I don't believe this is the proper place or time to discuss this. Now is the time to concentrate on the upcoming deployment."

No one else spoke for a while. They ate in silence, except for the sound of the silverware against the china. Osborne glanced at the men around him—a good group of men who knew how to fly and knew their jobs.

They finished the meal, and Osborne looked at his watch. "Let's assemble in front of the VOQ in about twenty minutes. Should be a van there to pick us up."

Osborne returned to his room, scanned it quickly, and then walked outside. He dropped his suitcase to the sidewalk and stood there watching the sky turn pink as the sun threatened to rise. The humidity was thick in the air, coating everything with a layer of sticky moisture.

The others joined him. Some sat on their suitcases. Two stood smoking, their cigarette tips glowing brightly in the gray of dawn. Still no one joked or talked.

The van, a big blue thing, pulled up. Osborne opened the back and tossed in his suitcase. He then climbed into the front seat as the rest of the men got in, sitting on the floor or the wheel covers or their suitcases. The ride to the briefing room was short. Shorter than he thought it should be. They left their gear in the van and entered the building. The air-conditioning contrasted to the humid outside air, chilling them.

They filed into the briefing room and took seats in the front, facing a raised stage. There was a screen on the wall, a slide projector on a table in front of it, and a lectern to one side. On one side stood the American flag and on the other that of South Vietnam—a yellow flag with three red stripes across the middle of it.

A moment later one man entered the room, dressed in starched jungle fatigues. The patches on his uniform were subdued—blacks and dark browns that didn't stand out. He wore a pistol on his hip, along with a canteen and a combat knife. Stage dressing to underscore the purpose of the briefing.

When he reached the lectern, he stopped and faced the men. "Gentlemen, my name is Major Kenneth Anderson, and I will be conducting this phase of the deployment briefing. The weather officer will be here shortly to give you a complete update on the nature of the weather for the first leg of the flight."

An airman entered the room, turned off the lights, and made his way to the slide projector. He turned that on and sat down behind it.

"Everything that I say from now on is classified secret and will not be discussed outside the confines of a secure area."

He nodded and the first slide appeared. It was a map of the United States with a bright red line drawn across it, through Alabama, Mississippi, Louisiana, Texas, New Mexico, Arizona, and California.

"Your flight route. Refueling points are marked." He noticed that Osborne and the others were beginning to take notes. He pointed down at them and said, "Don't worry about that. Maps, along with checklists, will be provided at the end of the briefing. This will be your last free ride for a while, so enjoy it."

The slide changed, and Anderson went into the details of the flight, giving them the flight information, altitudes, call signs for the tankers, and on and on. All the details that would normally be planned by the pilots themselves had been done for them. Headings, airspeeds, and checkpoints were all marked on the slides.

They went over the route of the flight, covering everything that the pilots would have to know. The weather officer, a young second lieutenant, came in and talked of fronts and winds aloft and reporting stations and high cirrus clouds. In the end he told them that the weather for the first leg of the flight, from Eglin to Hawaii, looked very good, but that weather over the Pacific was beginning to deteriorate and could present some problems for them later.

Others came in to talk to them. Platte arrived to tell them that they had done well during their brief stay at Eglin and that they were only the first of many who would be flying the Wild Weasel mission. He wished them luck and then disappeared out the side door.

The chaplain was the next man called. He prayed for them and with them for a few minutes and then hurried from the room. It was almost as if he was embarrassed by asking God for help in guiding the men to a war zone.

Anderson took over again and stood facing them for a moment. "There are many things that can be said at a time like this, but I think I'll resist the temptation. I'll wish you luck during your tour. I'll wish you good hunting. And I'll tell you that most men would say they wish they were going with you, but I'm not among them." He grinned broadly and added, "Better you than me."

There was a bark of laughter as the men realized that Anderson had been one of the few around to tell the truth. There would be those who claimed they wanted to go along, but none of them were volunteering for Vietnam. Anderson didn't want to go, and wouldn't volunteer, but when his turn came, he wouldn't drag his feet either.

Osborne stood up and said, "Thank you, Major, for your help this morning."

"Thank you," said Anderson.

Osborne surveyed his men and said, "Let's head on out to the flight line and get this show on the road."

Quietly, almost reluctantly, the men got to their feet and moved to the door.

From the time they had left the briefing room to the time they were airborne, nearly three hours had passed.

Takeoff time had come and gone as they worked to get everything ready. They had rolled the time back by thirty minutes and then forty-five, but that was all over now. They were up, airborne, in the nearly cloudless blue of the Florida sky, heading west, staying ahead of the sun.

Osborne sat there quietly, listening to the conversation on the radio—traffic between the control centers and the pilots of other planes, and talk from plane to plane as they cruised above the ground. Osborne was comfortable, relaxed, his fingers holding the stick, guiding it gently as he flew.

It was a quiet, relaxing time. High above the troubles of the world, wrapped in a metal cocoon, it was possible to eliminate all sound, all distractions, if he wanted to. A flip of the switch and the radios would fall silent. Not that it was a good idea to turn off the radios. The FAA would frown on that, especially since they were flying at about fourteen thousand feet, where all traffic was supposed to be on instrument flight rules. Each plane was supposed to be identified for the controllers, and each was supposed to be in radio contact.

He could turn the radios down so that they were barely audible. He would be alone, with the roar of the jet's engines behind him as he flew toward the west, toward Vietnam. Alone in his own world, at least for a couple of hours.

Thoughts of the morning, of getting ready for the flight, were overshadowed by the knowledge of where they were going. There had been briefings on the capabilities of the enemy's weapons. The SAMs couldn't lock onto a target under two thousand feet, but from ground level to two thousand feet there were other weapons. The ZSU-23/4, a multibarreled antiaircraft gun that was radar-controlled, could throw up a wall of lead. Firing thousands of rounds a minute, it could follow every move of a fighter, riddling it before the SAMs could be launched.

There were also larger weapons—37-millimeter and 57-millimeter. And there were smaller weapons. There was a 12.7 that the pilots in South Vietnam called the .51-caliber. It had an effective range of ten, eleven thousand feet and could shoot down a fighter as fast as anything the enemy had.

Osborne and his men had been warned that nearly every peasant, every farmer, every living person in North Vietnam had been given a weapon. AK-47s, SKSs, and M-1s were all over the north, and people would stand outside their hootches, firing at the jets. A well-placed, lucky shot could bring down a jet plane as fast as the most sophisticated weapons system.

There was even a story circulating that a helicopter had been shot down by a bow and arrow. More than one fighter had returned with arrows stuck in it. The enemy would shoot everything he could find at the planes, hoping to destroy one. A ridiculous situation.

But now, over the United States, there were not those worries. No one would be shooting at him. The only danger was from the weekend pilot who penetrated his airspace and flew into him. That had happened to others. It was rare, and usually the controllers saw the blip on the radar in time to warn everyone that there was unidentified traffic around.

Finally a call from the tanker broke into his thoughts.

He sat up straighter, checked the instruments again, and made a call back to the tanker.

"Have you on our scopes. Turn to a heading of 281. You are twenty miles out."

"Roger."

They made the rendezvous with the tanker, each plane filling its tanks. Then they pulled away and headed out to the west, flying high.

Nearly ten hours after takeoff from Eglin, the planes entered the traffic pattern at Hickam Air Force Base in Hawaii. They landed minutes later and taxied to the ramp where they would be refueled.

Osborne cracked the canopy, unbuckled his shoulder harness and seat belt, and then didn't move. He waited as the ladder was brought out and hung on the fuselage. As that was being done, he took off his helmet and hung it up. Then he raised his arms over his head, stretching.

As a crew chief climbed the ladder to look in, Osborne wiggled in his seat, trying to get the blood flowing. He'd been packed in there for over ten hours, his movements restricted by the equipment in the cockpit and the equipment he wore. As the crew chief retreated down the ladder, Osborne lifted himself from the seat and got out of the plane. Once on the ground, he stood there, arching his back, working out the kinks.

Kenyon, the man in the backseat, joined him and looked to the west, where black storm clouds were building.

"Looks like rain."

"Looks like it," agreed Osborne.

"If we're lucky, we could get weathered in and have to stay in Hawaii for a couple of days."

"Yeah, that would be a shame."

The other men, after getting out of their planes, began to drift across the ramp toward Osborne. A blue van like the one they had used in Florida came up and stopped short.

"Gentlemen, as you know, the flight ends here for the evening." Osborne pointed at the van that had stopped nearby. "As you can see, everything has been arranged. I suggest that we check into our quarters and then see about getting something to eat. Any questions?"

"Takeoff time tomorrow?"

Osborne looked at his watch and then at the sun, realizing that they were way off. It was the beginning of the afternoon in Hawaii, not the early evening it would be at Eglin Air Force Base in Florida.

"Our schedule calls for takeoff at 0900 hours." He stopped and tried a rapid calculation. "That's about two in the afternoon our time. A late takeoff, when you figure in the time zones."

"I can handle it."

Now Osborne grinned. "If any of you decide not to be in your room tonight, for whatever reason, please leave a number where you can be reached in case something happens."

"Yessir," answered one of the pilots.

With that they climbed into the rear of the van, and it took them to base operations. Osborne made sure that the planes would be refueled and that a maintenance crew would take a look at each one. That done, they all went back out to the van and climbed in to be taken to the VOQ.

Platte, or someone, had done all his homework. A block of rooms had been set aside for the men. Ten separate rooms, five on one side of the hall and five on the other. It made it simple to find everyone in the morning.

Osborne found that he could sleep that night. The VOQ was nicer than the one at Eglin—it had fans on the ceiling that spun fast enough to create a cool breeze. The quiet noise from it was relaxing and, before he knew it, his travel alarm was chirping at him.

He was up, feeling better than he had in days. He met with the others, ate another big breakfast, and then headed to operations. All the flight plans had been filed. It would be up to Osborne to open them as he taxied out to the runway. He finished the paperwork at operations and then walked out on the ramp where the aircraft waited.

Just as they had the day before, they preflighted, checking everything. That done, they loaded their gear and then waited for the time to begin engine run-up. The whole procedure was routine and, at nine o'clock, they were sitting on the taxiway waiting for permission to takeoff. That was granted, and they taxied onto the runway. A minute later, the wheels of the lead aircraft broke free of the ground, and it was airborne.

"You're off with everyone."

"Roger."

A few minutes later, with the flight joined, Osborne increased his cruising speed. They refueled in flight once and then landed at Anderson Air Force Base in Guam. In Hawaii, some of the men had gone out to party, figuring they had better get it in before they hit Vietnam. On Guam no one felt like having a party. They ate dinner in the officer's club and then, one by one, returned to their rooms to sleep. The long days of flying were taking a toll.

The next morning they ate breakfast together, went out to preflight together, and then waited together. They took off at nine in the morning, lifting into a sky that was gray, but there was no rain in it. Fifteen minutes later, they were above the cloud deck, heading for the last stop. Tan Son Nhut, Saigon, Republic of·Vietnam.

# ELEVEN

TAYLOR had nearly worn himself out. Or maybe it was closer to the truth to say that Linda had tried to wear him out. She had spent two minutes getting him out of his clothes and then had led him to the bed. She had pushed him down and begun shedding hers. They had ended in a pile beside the bed.

The activity had become a frenzy. First it had seemed that Linda could not be satisfied. She kept going, rubbing herself against Taylor's body as she kissed him, trying to get him interested in another session with her.

Taylor felt himself respond to her hands and lips. He rubbed a hand along her spine, feeling the light coating of sweat there. He thought about the textures of her skin, the smoothness and softness, and knew that he would be ready for her again, quickly.

And then he thought about airplanes blowing up over

North Vietnam. He thought about friends who wouldn't be coming back from the mission that he should have been leading. Suddenly he wasn't ready for her.

Without a word he stood up, turning his back to her. He moved to the window and looked out, down, on Saigon. He could see people circulating on the streets below him. Hundreds of people, moving through the neon light from the windows of the bars and clubs that catered to American servicemen. Americans walking hand in hand with Vietnamese women. Taylor didn't like that.

He turned and saw Linda, a Vietnamese woman, and suddenly didn't like her either. She was exploiting herself and him. Although she hadn't asked for money, she had made it clear that she was losing money by being with him. He was sure that she would expect a gift of money in the morning.

The sudden rage burned through him. He hated her and Vietnam and what he was doing. Not that he was in the hotel room, but that he was fighting a war that no one seemed to want but that somehow they had found.

Linda rolled to her back and put her hands under her head so that she was looking up at the ceiling. Then she looked at Taylor. Finally she asked, "What wrong?"

A dozen answers ran through his mind, but Taylor merely shook his head. "Nothing," he said.

"You come back here."

Taylor stared at her for a moment and then turned again, looking outside. He wasn't sure what he felt, but at that moment he knew he didn't want anything to do with a woman.

Linda apparently realized that Taylor needed to be left

alone. When Taylor looked at her, she hadn't moved, other than to cover herself with the sheet on the bed.

He moved back to the bed and sat down beside her. She didn't move until Taylor reached out and touched her on the shoulder. As she kissed the fingers of his hand, he felt the rage melt away, gone as quickly as it had come to him.

"What wrong?" she asked.

It was a question as old as warfare. Those not involved in combat didn't understand the emotions and the feelings of those who were. Those who stood on the sidelines, watching and listening, as Linda did, could sometimes almost understand. They were close enough to see things that the civilians and outsiders never did.

But Taylor didn't have an answer to her question. How could he tell her about his internal turmoil over the loss of his friends and the feeling that he had betrayed them? There were just some things that weren't said out loud except to other members of the fraternity. They could understand as no one else could.

Slowly he pulled the sheet down, exposing her naked body. The sweat had dried, but she still looked good, nearly perfect, at least to him.

She reached out, touched him, and pulled him to her. This time there was no hesitation, and no sudden memories distorted his view. He knew what he wanted and knew that she wanted it too.

As soon as he cracked the canopy on the taxiway, Osborne noticed a difference in the air. It was hot, humid, and filled with the stink of jet fuel. There was noise all around him—fighters winding up their engines, and the popping of rotorblades on helicopters. The ramp was not the clean, unobstructed area that it was on other bases, but was crowded with sandbagged revetments and corrugated-metal-covered Quonset-like huts to protect the aircraft from mortar and rocket shrapnel.

As far as he could see, there were aircraft parked. Fighters, old C-47s that were painted white and silver and belonged to the CIA, and helicopters and transports and spotter planes. Hundreds of aircraft, waiting for their chance to get into the war.

Following the instructions of the ground controllers, Osborne led his flight to a remote section of the ramp, where they parked. They were jockeyed into covered revetments and, as soon as they had shut down the engines, canvas tarps were dropped to hide the planes.

The men scrambled clear and stood on the ramp for a moment, waiting to see what would happen. Again, just like at Hawaii and Guam, a truck came for them, but instead of the blue crew van, this was an olive-drab Dodge truck that was open in the back. It stopped close to them, and Osborne glanced up at the driver, who turned out to be one of the men who had been assigned to the ground crew in the States.

"You made it, Donnelly."

Donnelly leaned out the window of the cab. "Couple of days ago, sir. We didn't get the opportunity to see the world. Stuck us in the back of a C-141 and brought us here via direct with hardly a chance to look out the windows."

Osborne laughed. "Those are the breaks."

"Yessir. Anyway, we've got things settled here and

got rooms for you all at the VOQ." He glanced at the rear, as if looking for a spy. "Some of the guys have already moved downtown."

"That allowed?"

"As long as we're back here by seven, no one cares what we do."

Osborne picked up his suitcase and tossed it into the rear of the truck. Before he climbed in, he said, "We need to run by operations first."

"Yessir."

Osborne climbed in and was followed by Kenyon. As Kenyon sat down, he said, "I would have thought that someone would be here to meet us."

"What for?"

"Welcome us to Vietnam."

"Maybe they couldn't find anyone with a sense of humor that warped."

As soon as everyone was in the truck, Osborne rapped the cab to let Donnelly know they were ready.

They lurched off, the diesel engine screaming, sounding like it was about to explode. They weaved their way through the revetments and parked aircraft until they came to a blacktopped road.

Osborne was surprised to see two-story barracks standing around them, making Tan Son Nhut look like almost every other military base he'd seen. Around the bottom floor was a wall of sandbags. Osborne wondered how they convinced anyone to live on the second floor.

They turned again and came to a long, low building. It had a peaked, metal roof that had rusted, turning it orange. There was a gravel parking lot around it with puddles from an afternoon rain. The top half of the wall was made of screen, and the bottom half was hidden by sandbags.

"Operations," said Donnelly.

Osborne climbed out of the truck and then said, "Pilots come with me. Donnelly, wait here."

They walked around to the front of the building and entered. Osborne stepped up to the waist-high counter and looked at the scheduling board, a white piece of plywood covered with acetate. The clerk had written the information in using a black grease pencil. Osborne noticed that the aircraft numbers of his planes were written in, but that no other information about them appeared on the board.

As Osborne moved to the counter, another man came toward him. He was dressed in starched jungle fatigues and looked like Anderson, at Eglin. The man held out a hand and said, "I'm Colonel Ott. Welcome to Vietnam."

"Major Osborne. Thank you, sir."

"Nothing to thank me for. I'd be writing to my congressman telling him about the rotten deal I'd gotten if I were you."

"Well," said Osborne, "General Augustine lost a son in Vietnam, and suddenly we have to deploy immediately."

"Ah," said Ott, "that explains quite a lot. Lieutenant Augustine was flying with our unit when he was killed."

"We heard missing," said Osborne.

"That's because we learned that one of the pilots had bailed out, but weren't sure who it was. We lost the four aircraft together so the information was a little sketchy. We've gotten word that it was Lieutenant Doyle who survived."

"I see, sir," said Osborne.

Ott turned and pointed to another man who stood near him. He looked tired, as if he hadn't gotten much sleep in the last few days. "This is Major Taylor. I just got him back from an in-country R and R and I don't think he got out of his room the whole time."

Taylor grinned weakly and said, "I've seen Saigon before. Didn't feel like seeing it again."

"Anyway," said Ott, "he'll be working as your liaison for the next few days, until you get settled in. Anything you want to know, you ask him."

Osborne knew the one question that everyone wanted answered. "What's the flying schedule look like?"

Ott rubbed his face with his hand and said, "Normally, we'd give you a week, ten days of easy missions and orientation flights. Stuff over South Vietnam and maybe into Cambodia or Laos." He shrugged, "But that probably won't do you any good, considering. Official briefing in the morning."

Taylor stepped forward. "First thing is to get you checked into the VOQ while we work on getting some quarters ready."

"Good," said Osborne. "I'd like it arranged so that all the officers can stay close together."

"Shouldn't be a problem." Taylor glanced at Ott. "Once we get that taken care of, we can head over to the Gunfighter's Club."

"And that is?"

"A club for the rated personnel. You have to have wings to get in. Doesn't matter if you're a pilot, navigator, or crew chief. If you have wings, you get in. If you're not rated, you don't."

"Sounds good."

Ott said, "I'll leave you here in Major Taylor's capable hands. I'll see you tomorrow at 0700." Ott retreated.

"We've got everything arranged now. Nothing to do but go on over to the VOQ, unless there's something you need to do here."

"I'm ready."

They left and climbed into the rear of the truck. Taylor gave Donnelly instructions and they drove over to the VOQ. As they stopped, Taylor said, "Get checked in, change clothes, shower, whatever, and I'll be back in an hour. We'll go to the club for dinner, and I can answer any questions you might have."

An hour later, at a big table in the corner of the Gunfighter's Club, Taylor and a number of pilots from the fighter squadron sat with the men from the Wild Weasels. They had ordered dinner—steaks, baked potatoes, and salad. There were bottles of beer sitting in front of everyone, and a bottle of bourbon sitting in the middle of the table that they passed around occasionally. The music had been turned down slightly, at Taylor's request, and the dancing girls had not appeared yet. He wanted to get a chance to talk to the new men before the distractions started.

The conversation wasn't very detailed because of the location. Osborne and his people could tell Taylor almost nothing about the Wild Weasel program and, in fact, refused to say the name out loud. Taylor could tell them nothing about the conditions over North Vietnam, other than to say it was rough and getting rougher.

They joked about flying, about the brass hats in the

Pentagon, East and West, and how it seemed that the military was no longer run by military leaders. It was run by managers. Taylor said that managers had never won a war. That was done by the leaders.

Before the debate could get started, the music was turned up and the first girl danced out onto the stage. She was wearing a one-piece flight suit that was so big she was nearly lost in it, but then she snaked down the zipper, revealing her undergarments, and the men began to cheer.

In a few minutes, she was naked, dancing around the stage, bending and bumping and grinding. She dropped to her back, lifted her legs, and spread them wide.

"This go on every night?" asked Osborne.

"Just about."

"Well, it beats old movies," said Osborne.

Taylor turned to look and then leaned close to Osborne. "But after a while it gets boring."

"Yeah." Osborne thought about the club they'd been to outside of Eglin where there had been a similar show. He wondered how he could have lived most of his life in cities where there had been no exotic dancers, no nudie shows, and then, once he joined the Air Force, could run into them everywhere. It didn't seem right that young men should be harassed in such a fashion, but then it was all a trick to separate the young men from their money. He wondered who was being exploited the most by the shows—the women who danced in them, or the young men who watched them dance.

Finally, having seen enough, Osborne said, "I think I'll head back to the room. Jet lag."

"Takes about a week to get over it. You'll find yourself dragging around by about five in the afternoon. If Ott was smart, he wouldn't get anything scheduled until middle of next week sometime."

Osborne drained his beer. "You say that as if we'll be flying soon."

"Probably sooner than you care to."

"Great." Osborne turned and looked at the stage. The dancer was on her feet. She had grabbed one ankle and lifted her leg slowly, keeping it straight until her foot was even with her ear. Then, slowly, she turned, giving everyone in the club a perfect view of her crotch.

"I've always wondered if the dancing turns them on," said Osborne.

"I knew one girl who would have danced for free," said Taylor. "Loved showing off her body that way, especially after her strict childhood. Made her feel as if she was sinful without really doing anything sinful."

"So one girl liked it," said Osborne.

"But she told me that most of them really don't care one way or the other. They make good money for very little work. The only drawback is that everyone thinks they're hookers, so they aren't treated very well."

"Better than getting shot at," said Osborne.

"Much."

"Okay. See you in the morning."

The morning briefing was not what Osborne had expected. All through training, and even in the operational units, they'd had inspections and training exercises and procedures. In each of those, there had been a routine that was followed precisely. It was laid out in the regulations and those regulations were rewritten and updated periodically. The inspectors used them to determine how well a unit would perform when deployed to a combat environment.

Now that he was in that combat environment, where there was a real enemy, not the invented enemy of a concocted scenario, he found that things were different. In the World, the intelligence briefing was a short program, giving some of the history of the conflict and then the capabilities of the enemy's weapons systems. Tactical maps were shown that had suspected triple-A and other antiaircraft sites marked on them. Airfields where enemy planes, usually MiGs, were located were in the center of concentric rings that showed the combat radius of the various planes stationed on them. No one ever paid attention, because it was all made-up information.

In those stateside briefings, the intel officer was the second man up because he had nothing to do with the real mission. The flight planning had to take into account the intel scenario, but that was only so that the inspectors knew that everyone was aware of it.

Here, in Vietnam, intel suddenly took on more importance. No longer was it an imaginary enemy firing imaginary bullets. It was a real enemy who had already shot down a number of American planes and killed a number of American pilots. The war was real.

Osborne sat in the intel briefing and suddenly wished that he had paid more attention when the intel officer was standing there talking about the enemy's capabilities. Multibarreled machine guns that were radar-driven were no longer an abstract horror but something he faced. Heat-seeking, radar-guided missiles would be flying up at him. It was no longer an irate rice farmer with a bolt-action rifle taking potshots at supersonic jets, but sophisticated weapons that could fill the sky with lead and steel.

And to make it even worse, Osborne and his pilots were going out to look for the enemy. They wanted the enemy to shoot at them so that they could locate the enemy's command centers and shut them down or blow them up.

"Shit!" he said to himself.

The slide being shown, taken by a recon aircraft, displayed one of the many SAM sites used by the North Vietnamese. The intel officer described the interlocking and overlapping fields of fire that made the missiles effective from the ground up to nearly eighty or ninety thousand feet.

The next slide showed a drawing of a site, with the missile launch areas, the radar vans, the control center, and the maintenance areas all marked.

"Take out the radars, and the site is blind. They can shoot with the visually sighted weapons, but everything else is down. The site is no longer a major threat."

With that, the intel officer showed a map of North Vietnam. The SAM sites were marked in red, airfields with MiGs in orange, heavy concentrations of triple-A in yellow. The area around Hanoi and Haiphong seemed to glow with color. Other areas had sparse defenses, but nearly all the country had some, even if it was only optically sighted triple-A.

When he had finished his briefing, he asked, "Any questions?"

Osborne felt that he should have a dozen, but could think of nothing. The ranges of the various weapons had been given, the effective ranges of the SAMs had been noted, and the target to be attacked had been specified.

Ott took the stage when the intel officer was finished. He flashed a map of North Vietnam up on the screen and said, "Flying in combat is different from anything else you new men might have experienced. In combat, anything goes and regulations sometimes get lost."

He leaned on the lectern, staring down at Osborne and his men. "Let me clarify that. A combat situation can put strains on a man that aren't found elsewhere. Back in the World, regulations prohibit flying below one hundred feet AGL. In combat, to survive, you sometimes have to fly at ten feet."

He grinned. "In training, as a fighter pilot, you learn how to engage enemy aircraft. If you find yourself in a training situation, armed only with air-to-surface rockets, then you would be considered a casualty and the scoring would go against you. Not too long ago a pilot found himself in that situation. Armed only with air-to-surface rockets and being attacked by a MiG. He hit the enemy with his rockets and has credit for the kill."

"Christ," said Kenyon.

"The point is that you have to remain flexible. The situation is changing, fluid, and you have to flow with it. Now, according to the information and briefing materials that I've received, I know that some of your equipment is experimental. We'll have to check it out." He glanced down at Osborne.

"Yes, sir," said Osborne. "There was no way to check it all on the ground at Eglin before we deployed."

"Fine," said Ott. "What I want to do is put you men

up in a mission on route package one. That is the south-ernmost of the North Vietnam runs. There's little in the way of triple-A and SAM threats, but enough that you can get your feet wet, check your equipment out, and get back here before we go after something farther north."

"Why not just head in full bore?" asked Kenyon.

Osborne wanted to ring the youngster's neck for him and turned in his seat to glare at him. He was about to say something, when Ott answered the question in full using the information that Osborne had supplied to him only a few minutes earlier.

"First, we always send the new men out on route one. Gives them a taste of what happens, but not with the intensity of a mission farther north. It lets you see what the war is like without the entire North Vietnamese Army trying to shoot your ass out of the air.

"And second, there are enough triple-A and SAM complexes around that we can find out if the equipment and the theory work right. If you go farther north and discover that some part of the theory is wrong, we might lose everything. We need to have a chance to recover."

"Yes, sir."

"If there are no other questions, I'll turn this briefing over to the operations officer and let him talk for the rest of the briefing."

Osborne leaned back in the wicker chair and watched the operations officer take the stage. Osborne still wasn't happy with the direction things had taken, with the mission being seen as one more training exercise, but with the enemy gunners thrown in as an added bonus attraction. Now, at least he understood why he had ended up in South Vietnam and not staging out of Thailand like many of the other Air Force missions. General Augustine was making sure that the men who flew with his boy had the chance to get even for him.

But, as he thought about it, he decided it was a good idea. If the intelligence boys at Eglin had been wrong about the radars and frequencies used, it would be nice to know before they reached Hanoi, with the sky full of flak and missiles.

Besides, who wanted to get into a war anyway? People got killed in wars, and Osborne had already learned about short timers and going home in a box. Each day marked off meant he was one day closer to rotating home, and that was all that counted in Vietnam. Living long enough to go home.

He shifted around and listened closely as the operations officer began to explain the mission, the ingress and egress routes for a target they had hit before but had failed to destroy. Today would be different because they had new protection. They could concentrate on the target while the men flying Wild Weasels concentrated on suppressing the enemy gunners.

Osborne smiled to himself. At the very least it would be interesting. He had no doubt about that.

# TWELVE

AIRBORNE, near Yankee Station in the South China Sea, Osborne was relaxed. They had just finished with the tanker and had turned toward the coast of North Vietnam. Taylor had acknowledged Osborne's call, and that they were now on the way to North Vietnam.

As they approached the coastline, they reached the leading edge of a storm with a line of clouds that stretched from a point near the DMZ and Khe Sanh northeast toward Haiphong harbor. Over the South China Sea it was a clear, sunny day. Over North Vietnam it was overcast, with the cloud ceiling dropping the farther west it got. There were thunderstorms associated with the front. Everyone could hear the bursts of static that filled the radio as the lightning flashed somewhere along the storm front to the west of them.

Osborne heard, for the first time, the pilots in other flights making their radio calls. He listened to them for a moment, fascinated because it sounded like the chatter that he'd heard a hundred other times on a hundred training missions. Men joking with one another or calling the flight they had joined or warning the leader of trouble around them. The words—bingo, bandit, tallyho, and no joy, words that he'd used himself—took on an added significance because of the location. They were now flying over North Vietnam.

Staying close to Taylor's flight, Osborne didn't understand why they were just under the cloud deck. He would have preferred to be above it, out of sight from the enemy on the ground. The closer to the ground they got, the higher the fuel consumption. But then, Osborne didn't know all the factors involved and assumed that Taylor had a good reason for staying under the clouds.

As they moved deeper into North Vietnam, he heard someone call, "Weasel, I have a single ringer."

That meant that someone—Osborne didn't recognize the voice and would have to warn everyone to use call signs—had picked up the first indication of a SAM radar tracking them.

"Say call sign."

"Weasel three."

"Wasp, we have SAM indications to the west. Distant."

"Roger."

From somewhere else came, "Turkey, we have MiG-19s at three o'clock."

Osborne looked in that direction, but could see nothing other than clouds and more clouds. They were just under the deck, where the grays and blacks of the storm were swirling around them.

"Guns at two o'clock."

"Say ID."

"Weasel two. Guns at two o'clock. Weak indication."

"Roger."

"Coming up on IP," said Taylor.

"Weasel has a double ringer. Weasel three."

And then, almost immediately, "Weasel four has a triple ringer at eight o'clock."

"Weasels, let's bend it around," said Osborne. For some reason he had been reluctant to initiate the attack. Weak indications of the enemy radar meant the sites were distant, but now they had one up, behind them.

"Guns at one o'clock."

"ID."

"Weasel three."

Osborne didn't want to break the flight apart and attack more than one target, but then, he was set up with two elements. Three could take out the guns while he went after the SAM. Indications were from SAM Fan Song radars and gun Fire Can radars.

"Take the guns, Weasel three."

"Got it. Breaking off."

Over the ICS, Kenyon said, "Got a strong indication. That son of a bitch stays on the air, we've got his ass."

Osborne lined up on the radar signal, using it to guide his plane. He dived toward the ground, away from the cloud deck behind him.

"Guns at ten o'clock."

Osborne glanced in that direction and saw the muzzle flashes of the big weapons as they began to fire at him.

Clouds of smoke billowed upward and the flak began to burst around him. Tiny puffs of smoke that he ignored.

He turned his attention back to the SAM site, flipping the switches on the instrument panel to arm the rockets. They entered a light rain, the mist obscuring the ground and the objects on it.

"We got a launch!"

"Where?"

Over the radio came, "Launch! Launch!"

Osborne saw nothing. He steepened the dive and rolled to the right. He saw the flame from the rear of the missile as it turned toward him. Osborne counted, dived, and then climbed. The missile tried to follow as Osborne turned inside it and then climbed upward. He rolled over and started down again, aiming at the SAM sight.

"Triple ringer," said Kenyon, from the backseat.

"Where?" shouted Osborne.

"Nine o'clock."

Osborne turned left, into the site. He dropped the nose, diving at the site, trying to line up on it. He saw it through the mist and opened fire. The rockets from the jet leaped out, tiny flames burning, leaving trails of dark smoke. They seemed to scatter downward, toward the SAM site.

A moment later there were explosions on the SAM site. Flashes of light and geysers of dirt erupted upward. One of the missiles toppled from its launcher, fire spreading along it. Men were running away, out into the open fields, leaving the site behind them.

"All right!" shouted Osborne, broadcasting by mistake.

As he pulled up, climbing out, he glanced to the rear, twisting around as his wingman opened fire. The first of his rockets landed in the center of the site, where the radar vans and command vehicles were parked.

"Got another Fan Song," shouted Kenyon. "Two o'clock, strong signal."

Osborne rolled toward it but couldn't see a thing. The rain was getting heavier and they were closer to the ground. No more than a hundred, maybe a hundred and fifty feet above it.

"Vector scope looks like a Christmas tree," yelled Kenyon, the excitement creeping into his voice.

Over the radio came, "Got a SAM launch. I can't see it. Anyone see the SAM?"

"Three is breaking down and to the right."

"Where's the SAM?"

Now Osborne was getting worried. He was looking around wildly, trying to spot the flash of fire that marked a SAM, but at a hundred and fifty feet he wouldn't have time to react if the missile suddenly locked on him and dived from above.

"Guns," shouted Kenyon.

As he did, Osborne saw the tracers rocket by the cockpit—glowing red balls that disappeared into the cloud deck. He rolled over and hit the trigger for the cannons. He thought that he could feel the weapons firing and watched as the rounds walked through the gun emplacement. It stopped firing as something down there exploded. Osborne hauled over on the stick to avoid the expanding ball of flame.

All around him the ground was erupting—men shooting upward as the Wild Weasels dived on the targets. Rockets tore up the ground as the 20-millimeter cannons chewed up real estate. There was return fire and then a secondary explosion.

"I got a double ringer to the right. Weasel four."

Osborne had no idea where Weasel four was. The flight had gotten separated by the enemy. He pulled back on the stick and climbed high, toward the cloud deck. Once close, he eased off and turned, looking back the way he'd come. Through the mist and the fog, he could see a couple of fires burning but couldn't see the other two jets.

"Got a ringer at four o'clock," said Kenyon.

Without thinking, Osborne turned toward it.

"Double ringer."

He pushed on the stick, starting his dive toward the SAM site.

"Triple ringer."

Again he used the cannons as the site came into view. The rounds chewed through the berm surrounding one of the launch buds on the complex. They hit the missile, tearing through it. Smoke poured from its side. Osborne jinked right and the rounds hit one van.

"Signal is still strong," said Kenyon.

Osborne broke off his attack as his wingman hit the site, first with rockets that exploded near the trailers parked close to the center. Two men dived out of one as it began to burn, the flames leaping high.

Osborne began another climb and turned in the direction of the Wasp flight. He rolled out but couldn't see the planes. "Wasp leader, where are you?"

"IP inbound."

"What's it look like back there, Kenyon?"

"Weak guns to the right, about four o'clock. Nothing else. Board is clean."

"Shit. What happened?"

Kenyon shrugged, his eyes glued to the threat board in front of him. "Don't know. They must have shut down the radars. They do that, we can't see them."

"That's fine with me," said Osborne, "because then they can't see us. They can't see us, they can't shoot us." He glanced at the chart on his knee board, looking for the IP. It was fifty miles to the west.

"Weasel flight, join on me."

"Roger."

A moment later Weasel four said, "We're all here. You can get moving."

"Hit the burners."

They took off, racing just under the cloud deck, toward the IP. After forty miles, in the distance, Osborne could see four specks that he hoped were the Wasp flight. He turned toward them and said, "Wasp, I'm at your five o'clock."

"Got you."

"Got a ringer," said Kenyon.

"Where?"

"At our eleven o'clock. This is a new one. Guy just came up. There he goes."

"Out of burner," said Osborne.

The flight slowed. For a moment everything was calm. No one was shooting at anyone, there were no MiGs in the air around them, and there were no indications that any of the enemy radar systems were on.

Osborne took a deep breath and realized that his body hurt. He'd been sitting in the same position, tensed, for nearly thirty minutes. His shoulders ached, his legs hurt, and his hand was cramped. Sweat had drenched his body, leaving him feeling clammy, uncomfortable. He wished that he could scratch his back or the bottoms of his feet. Funny how the bottoms of the feet began to itch.

"Wasp, rolling in," said Taylor.

Osborne watched the fighter-bombers start their run. At first there didn't seem to be any enemy around. Then the sky filled with tracers, easy to see against the gray mist of the light rain.

And as the fighters began their run in, the radars all came up. Kenyon called the sightings, right, left, and in front. Osborne kept his eyes outside the cockpit, searching the ground. There was a cluster of hootches in front of him, and in the center of them was a single radar antenna. The enemy had tried to disguise it, but the antenna itself had to stay clear. If they covered it, it became worthless.

As the guns around the site began to fire, Osborne rolled over, diving toward the van. When the sights lined up, the pipper centered, he opened fire. The van seemed to vibrate under the impact of the 20-millimeter rounds.

"Lost the site," said Kenyon.

But as he spoke, another came up strong. Before he could say anything they were in a steep bank.

"Got the missiles," yelled Osborne.

He'd spotted the camouflage net that concealed them. The enemy must have planned to fire the missile through the netting, figuring that it wouldn't adversely affect the missile's flight.

As he lined up on the site and opened fire, the cannon shells walked in, over the berm, across a missile, and out again. Flames spread, engulfing the weapon. Thick, black smoke began to climb into the gray mist.

Behind him his wingman did the same thing, attacking the site to the left of his run. He hit the radar van, the command van, and a repair shop. There were two secondary explosions, and the fire began to spread rapidly, even in the light rain.

"Lost the ringer," said Kenyon.

"Yeah," said Osborne. He hauled back on the stick and climbed rapidly. He rolled to the right, took a look at the SAM site. Even the camouflage netting was on fire. Flames had spread from one area into another, setting a second missile on fire. There was an explosion and the missile launched itself along the ground. It hit the berm, flipped up, and then crashed into the ground like a bottle rocket gone mad. Finally it collided with a shed, and there was a white flash and a rolling cloud of gray that engulfed most of the site.

With that site down, even the gun radar had gone off the air, and Osborne turned again, trying to catch the flight of fighters, which were beginning their attacks on the target.

Taylor, his flight racing just under the cloud deck, trying to avoid any MiGs sent up, knew that the target was close. They'd tried to knock out the small rail complex near Tuyen Hoa a couple of times. The enemy knew that it was a target, so they had moved in the triple-A and the SAMs to defend it. No sense in wasting air-defense capabilities on a target the Americans weren't going to attack.

As he lined up to head into the target, there was no one shooting at him yet. All the firing had been directed toward the Weasels, and it seemed that the enemy had already discovered that the Weasels were drawn to the radar vans. Turn off the radars and the Weasels stayed away.

Taylor saw the rail yards in front of him, in the distance. Ribbons of steel and ties led north and south. The rain masked part of it, but didn't hide it completely. Taylor knew they could drop bombs on the tracks for hours and still not sever the hub. They might make routing through the yard difficult, but it would still be usable.

After studying the photos, Taylor had decided to take out the buildings and a series of bridges to the north, and ignore the yard itself. If there was any rolling stock, he hoped to destroy it, especially any locomotives that might be around. Those were the targets of opportunity.

As he rolled in, the main building complex in front of him, the firing began. Flak burst around him, the gunners guessing at his altitude by measuring from the base of the cloud deck. They weren't coming close.

Taylor flipped the switches, arming the weapons systems, and then pickled the bombs. As they came free, arcing toward the target, he hauled back on the stick, climbing out, heading for the clouds above him.

Tracers from several weapons flashed past him, but none of them were close either. Taylor stayed in the climb, wondering if he should just disappear into the clouds. There was a possibility of MiGs on top, but no one had mentioned them for quite a while. The AWACS had yet to alert anyone about anything.

Taylor stayed in the climb, upward into the swirling gray soup of the clouds, and then was suddenly out, into the brightness of the sun. He leveled off and turned again, heading toward the South China Sea. As he did, he said, "Wasp, check."

"Two."

"Three."

"Four."

"What'd it look like back there, four?"

"Part of two bridges down, fires in the rail yards with some of the cars burning. Heavy smoke."

"Roger," said Taylor. "Weasels."

"Weasel, go."

"Roger. We're on top now, heading for the barn. You are welcome to join us up here."

"Roger."

As Osborne answered, Kenyon was on the ICS. "Got a double ringer. Gone to triple. At eleven o'clock."

That was a new one. Osborne turned toward it but could see nothing. Too much rain now. He dropped down, to the deck, aiming his jet at the SAM site. He raced across the rice paddies and popped up, over the lines of trees. To one side were columns of black smoke from the burning railroad yard.

This time, Osborne didn't have much left. He'd fired all the rockets and most of the 20-millimeter ammunition. He was sure that the other Weasels had done the same.

"Give me a pepper report."

"Two's down to twenty Mike Mike."

"Ditto three."

"And four."

From the backseat came, "Lost him. He's off the air."

Osborne was tempted to climb up, through the clouds, and join with Taylor and the Wasps. Get out now. It had been a good mission and the questions had been answered. The Weasel mission would work and it would work well.

Still there was a missile site somewhere around them. They knew about where it was, and it seemed a shame to let the enemy have one that hadn't been attacked.

"Are we close to bingo?" asked Osborne.

"Two's good."

"And three."

"And four."

"He's up again," said Kenyon.

"Give me a vector," said Osborne.

"Come right about three degrees and you should see him in the distance."

Osborne did as he was told and pointed himself at the enemy missile sight. He began a slight climb, gaining altitude slowly. The enemy gunners, those with AKs and 12.7s, began to fire, their green and white tracers cutting through the mist and the rain. Glowing emeralds and shiny snowballs that looked harmless, almost like fireworks from the Fourth of July. They weren't close to the flight.

And then, in the distance, he saw the berm of the SAM site—one of the hills, five, six, seven feet tall, that protected the missiles from fighter attack. Over the top he could see the nose of the SA-2, a pointed thing with tiny guidance fins on the front of it. There were wings further back that were not for lift but for stability.

As he saw the weapons, he opened fire, watching as the 20-millimeter rounds hit the berm, blowing through it and throwing clods of dirt into the sky. It looked almost like mud splashing upward.

As he crossed the top of the site, he rolled his aircraft once in a victory salute. When he righted himself, he began a rapid climb, heading for the protection of the clouds.

Behind him, his number-two man saw the radar van —it was tucked into the center of the complex, protected by the berm and a grove of palm trees. He opened fire on it, riddling it as he passed overhead and then into his victory roll before joining with the leader, climbing into the sky.

"He's down again," reported Kenyon.

"I got the radar," said two.

"Weasels, let's get out of here. Join on me and hit the burners."

Osborne aimed for the clouds, popped through them in a few seconds, and then leveled off. In the distance he could see the flight of F-105s as they headed out toward the South China Sea.

A few minutes later, as Osborne and his flight caught up with Taylor, Osborne said, "Out of burner. Give me a check."

"Two."

"Three."

"Four."

"Roger. Wasp lead, I'm behind you at your seven o'clock. The threat board is clean."

"Roger. We're on our way home."

"Roger." Osborne relaxed then. The mission was as good as over. He wiggled in the seat, trying to get comfortable. His muscles ached from the strain of sitting in one position for so long. They ached from the constant strain of waiting for the aircraft to burst apart. They ached from the feeling that a bullet was going to hit him in the back of the head.

But he was elated, too. They had taken a concept that no one was sure would work in combat and put it to the test. Not the simple test that everyone had thought, but a tough one with missile sites and triple-A all over the place. A thorough test of the system, and the only thing wrong was that they couldn't carry enough ordnance to attack everyone who needed it. They'd left several sites burning, missiles destroyed, but there was more to be done.

As they crossed the coastline of North Vietnam and pushed out over the South China Sea toward the refueling tanker, Osborne felt all the tension drain out of him. Now the worst that could happen was an aircraft crash, the plane falling apart because of shoddy maintenance. He wasn't worried about that. It was something that no pilot ever worried about. When they reached the South China Sea, they were safe.

"Weasels," said Taylor, "that was an outstanding job. I'll be buying the beer."

"That go for everyone?" asked one of the Wasp pilots.

"Goes for the Weasels and everyone who hit the target," said Taylor. "You'll need the BDA before I buy everyone a drink."

"I'll get the lab boys to run the film as soon as we get back."

"Roger."

"And two minutes later, I'll be in the club looking for my drink."

"Let's knock off the chatter," said Taylor.

"Not until I tell you about the beautiful explosion that wiped out the locomotive that entered just as my bombs hit. That's worth more than a beer."

"I think we deserve a keg, at the very least."

"Maybe two, with the dancing girls sitting with us."

"Tonight, while we're young enough to enjoy it."

"I said knock off the chatter." Taylor's voice cut through the other transmissions, washing them out. He repeated it again and again until there was silence on the radio. When he had it, he said, "I'll buy the first round tonight. And the third and the fifth. Someone else is going to have to take the even ones."

Osborne was feeling so good about what had happened that he didn't think his way through the problem. He just said, "I've got the even ones."

"And I'll talk to the girls," said someone else.

"We party tonight!"

# THIRTEEN

LIEUTENANT General Clarence Augustine sat facing the windows of his huge office. Those in the room with him could only see the rear of his high-backed chair. No one spoke, knowing the pain the general was suffering. Knowing the inner turmoil of a man who had lost his only son.

Colonel Platte knocked on the outer door but didn't wait for an answer from inside. He entered, glanced at the three men sitting on the couch and at the back of the general's chair. He raised his eyebrows in question.

One of the men answered by pointing. He didn't speak either.

In the background the radio played quietly, the music rock and roll. Platte was surprised that the general would be listening to rock and roll, and then decided that it must be a tribute to his son.

"General," said Platte quietly. When there was no answer, he said it again, louder.

Slowly the chair turned. Platte was surprised to see how old the general looked. He had aged ten, twenty years in the space of a couple of days. His face was deeply lined and his eyes were red. The general had been mourning the death of his son, and there was no one who didn't understand.

"General, I have reports from Vietnam. First reports from Vietnam."

"Yes?"

Platte glanced at the three men, all majors and above. To get a commission on active duty required that each man have a security clearance. To work with the general probably meant that they all had top-secret clearances. The Wild Weasels was a classified program. Only those with a need to know about them were supposed to know about them.

But there were times when the considerations of the country took a backseat to the considerations of the individual. He didn't want to pass the information along with the three men listening, but then, he didn't want to make life harder for the general.

Ignoring the three men, he said, "I have the first after-action reports from our special unit."

"Maybe it would be better to wait," said the middle man on the couch.

"No," snapped the general. "I want to hear this."

Platte glanced at the men, but the general didn't pick up on the gesture. Platte then shrugged and said, "Preliminary reports claim a major success. SAM sites were kept from firing, and the bombing mission went in almost untouched."

The general didn't react right away.

Platte waited and then gave out the details, explaining everything that had happened, including the number of sites that had been attacked and the suspected number of missiles destroyed.

"It was an unqualified success."

The general slammed a hand onto his desk top and then dropped his head to his hand. He was quiet for a long time, not moving, not speaking. Platte stood in front of the desk, watching the man, wondering what he was thinking.

Finally Augustine looked up and said, "Did we take any casualties?"

"No, sir. I think we caught them flat-footed. Minimal damage to the airframes and no one wounded."

"Good. Good. I was worried that we had deployed the men too early. Too quickly, without the training they should have had before they deployed."

"General," said Platte, "the first mission was into the area where . . . ah, where the disaster took place. Lots of triple-A and SAMs. Our people got in and out. Got even."

Augustine stared up at Platte and said, "It is not good tactics to worry about getting even. Getting even is not a military mission."

Platte didn't know what to say. He had been told never to argue with a general because the general would always win. But sometimes, the general didn't have all the information available. Sometimes it was necessary to provide all the information so that a rational decision could be made.

"Getting even is what it's all about. We show them that they can do anything they want as long as they're willing to take the casualties. Sometimes we have to prove to them that if they make us mad enough we're going to stomp them into the ground and then grind the ashes into dust."

"I wouldn't want to think that those other boys flew into jeopardy so that I could get even."

"Oh, no, sir," said Platte. "They flew the mission to stomp the shit out of the enemy. Show him that we can only be pushed so far, and then we get mad."

Augustine stared at Platte for a long time, studying him. Finally he said, "Thank you, Colonel. Is there anything else that you need to tell me?"

Platte stood there for a moment, his mind racing. He wanted to say something to the general, to let him know that he understood the turmoil, the sorrow, but he could think of nothing. He didn't know the general that well, didn't know what he could say to him.

"No, sir, that takes care of it."

"Thank you. Thank you for taking the time to come here."

"No problem, General." He had almost said that he was glad to do it, but didn't.

"Oh," said the general. "What's being done for the boys who flew the mission?"

"I'm afraid that I don't understand."

"Has anyone written them up for awards? Have any citations been submitted?"

"Sir, the mission is still classified. It's next to impossible to submit any names for an award."

The general nodded. "I understand. I want you to contact the unit commander and have him order a case of beer for each and every man on that flight. And have him get some steaks for them. Bill me for it."

"Yes, General."

"It's little enough for me to do."

Platte nodded, and asked, "Will there be anything else, General?"

"That's it. Thank you again."

Platte saluted, executed the first about-face he'd done since West Point, and got out.

As the wheels touched the runway at Tan Son Nhut, Osborne wanted to shout. He wanted to get out and leap into the air. He wanted to pound the other pilots and EWOs on the back and tell them that everything was just fucking great.

He taxied slowly, fighting the urge to rush. He parked the aircraft, in the revetment, away from the prying eyes of the enemy, and then threw off his shoulder harness and seat belt. As soon as the ladder touched the side of the aircraft, he was down it, hurrying across the tarmac.

The other Weasel pilots were on the ground, too. Three of them stood near the tail of one of the jets. They were laughing and slapping each other on the back.

"Oh, yeah, fucking beautiful. *Beau-ti-ful!*" yelled one of them.

Just as Osborne arrived, Taylor roared up in a jeep. In one hand he held a bottle of champagne. As the jeep rolled to a stop, he leaped out.

"That was absolutely the greatest thing I've ever seen. Kept the triple-A and the SAMs off us so we could complete our mission."

He untwisted the wire around the bottle's neck, pulled it free, and stuck it into his pocket. He didn't want to leave anything around that could be sucked into a jet engine. He popped the cork and sent the driver after it as the wine poured from the top of the bottle.

Taylor took a long pull at it and then held the bottle aloft. "Gentlemen, congratulations."

Osborne grabbed the bottle and drank. When he finished, he handed it to Kenyon, who was standing right beside him. They passed it around until everyone had taken a drink.

"My number four," said Taylor, "told me that we hammered the target. Blew the shit out of it and destroyed a couple of locomotives. We were able to put everything onto the target because we didn't have to worry about the SAMs."

"We made that much of a difference?"

"Hell, yes. The SAMs were so busy worrying about you guys that they didn't have time for us. We laid the bombs right on the targets."

"We have BDAs yet?"

"One of my guys ran the film over to the lab as soon as they got the camera pulled. We'll have that in less than an hour, but hell, we saw the rail yard on fire. I saw the railroad bridge collapse. We got them good."

"Then I think we should celebrate," said Osborne.

A second jeep approached, and Ott climbed out. He looked at the bottle of champagne and said, "Let's not have too much drinking on the flight line."

"Never, sir," said Taylor.

"I just got the preliminaries on the mission," said Ott. "Looks like we've got a winner."

"Which means?" asked Osborne.

Ott shook his head and grinned. "That you did your job too well. You made too big a difference and your reward is going to be more missions over the north."

"Well, shit!" said Osborne.

"I'll drink to that," said Taylor, as he passed the bottle around again.

Osborne would never admit it, but he was proud of the job. It wasn't everyone who got to try a new mission in combat and have it work so well.

"Give me the bottle," he said. "I'm going to need a big drink."

"You take it," said Ott. "You deserve it. All your men deserve one."

Osborne looked at the colonel and decided that he was right. They did deserve it.

# There's an epidemic with 27 million victims. And no visible symptoms.

It's an epidemic of people who can't read.

Believe it or not, 27 million Americans are functionally illiterate, about one adult in five.

The solution to this problem is you...when you join the fight against illiteracy. So call the Coalition for Literacy at toll-free **1-800-228-8813** and volunteer.

## Volunteer Against Illiteracy. The only degree you need is a degree of caring.

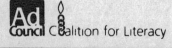

Ad Council    Coalition for Literacy